LIES AND DEATH

PAM CLIFFORD

To Paul and Steven

CHAPTER 1

Saturday 8th October

Amanda was excited to be seeing Valerie again. It seemed ages since the coach tour of Italy when they had got on so well, and when the new brochure from Tour2Explore Holidays landed on her doormat last week, she didn't think twice. She emailed Valerie and suggested meeting up to arrange another holiday. She didn't have to wait long for the enthusiastic reply, and today they were meeting to discuss where they would like to go.

She had hoped to meet in her friend's home town of Bath, a city she loved and hadn't visited for some time, but Valerie had preferred Stow on the Wold as she had fond childhood memories of the place, and she could call on a relation in nearby Chipping Norton afterwards.

Amanda suggested they meet outside the White Hart, which was easy to locate in the town square. By arriving early she'd managed to get a good parking space, and enjoyed a gentle stroll into the centre. The sun was warm so she decided to make the most of it and wait on one of the benches situated on the green, from where she could easily see the meeting point and enjoy a spot of people watching.

She looked at her watch and found she still had a little time to kill, so reached into her tote bag and took out the brochure, leafing through to the page for the holiday she'd chosen – a full two weeks travelling across Europe to Croatia. She had always wanted to visit Dubrovnik, and the waterfalls at the Krka National Park looked amazing in the photos.

The church clock struck eleven and there was still no sign of her blonde friend. She shouldn't really be surprised as punctuality hadn't been Valerie's best attribute. On holiday she'd often float into dinner at least ten minutes after everyone else was seated. Amanda smiled at the memory of the Single Six, as their little group had been named. As all the other passengers were couples they'd all been directed to the same table on the first night and had enjoyed each other's company at mealtimes from then on.

After a while the wooden slats of the bench were becoming uncomfortable so she rose and strolled over to the hotel, stopping to look into a shop where some pretty scarves swayed in the light breeze by the door, but there wasn't time now to linger. She walked on to the meeting point by a big open gateway, and watched as a local bus pulled in by the town hall, and passengers filed off to be replaced by those waiting. A few minutes later, the bus left by the same route from which it had arrived.

Amanda's back was now aching from standing in one place so she wandered a few yards further. Another quick look at her watch told her it was now eleven thirty. This was late even by Valerie's standards and Amanda was beginning to get worried. Where was her friend? Was she coming? Had something happened to her?

There was a café across the road with a large bow window. Rummaging in the bottom of her bag, she pulled out her phone and sent a quick text to let Valerie know where she would be, then hesitated, as if expecting it to ring. It didn't.

Pleased to see that a window table was free, she opted for a coffee and couldn't resist treating herself to a scone with jam and cream. She tried to make her snack last as long as possible, but it soon became apparent that, as lunchtime was drawing near and the small tearoom was filling up, she ought to vacate her table. Once she'd paid and dropped a coin from her change into the tips jar, with increasing frustration she left the premises. A group of tourists were spilling out of a coach nearby which only enhanced her frustration as she thought of the holiday she may not have now.

She sent another text, but when there was still no reply, set off slowly around the square, giving her friend one last chance to turn up before calling it a day. She purchased some rather decadent hand-made chocolates, read the small ads outside the newsagents, and finally returned to the shop where she'd seen the scarves earlier and bought one that particularly appealed – a treat to brighten a disappointing day. It was time to resign herself to the fact that Valerie just wasn't coming. She trudged through an alleyway to the back street where she had parked her little Fiat and, feeling totally deflated, headed home.

CHAPTER 2

Saturday 8th October

The sun was only just peeping over the horizon when Alan placed his golf clubs into the boot of his elderly Toyota. The weather forecast for the Peak District was good and he was looking forward to a full eighteen holes with his old student mates. It had been a while since he'd seen them. Jack lived furthest away and was collecting Mark en route while Fred would be driving in from a different direction. The last time they had all been together was the summer they graduated when they had jetted off to the Costa de Sol for the summer to play golf, living alongside cockroaches in a grotty flat in Torremolinos, and working in bars to finance the venture. It all seemed like a lifetime away now.

Sitting high up on the escarpment, the popular Wellsend Golf Club had panoramic views and Alan was sure his mates would be impressed. He was proud to be the golf professional at this club and really enjoyed his job. He parked up and didn't have long to wait before he saw the unmistakable custom paintwork of Jack's camper van as it swung into the narrow lane.

Jack stretched dramatically as he stepped out of his vehicle.

"Wow – what a view!"

Mark, who had spent the summer as a holiday rep in the Algarve and looked really tanned and fit, strode over to Alan and gave him a big hug. "Beautiful part of the world, this. I've missed seeing green fields!" He stepped back to look his friend up and down. "You're looking well on married life."

"Thanks, mate. I could do with losing a few pounds though." Alan patted his tum.

The three friends chatted easily together as they stood looking out at the view, only unloading their golf bags from their vehicles when they realised the sound of a very noisy exhaust was gradually getting nearer. Surprised to see their mate Fred clambering out of the old rust bucket of a Ford Fiesta, they wandered over to meet him.

Rather embarrassed, Fred explained, "Dad borrowed my car last night. I think he wanted to impress a new lady friend, and it must have done the trick because he hadn't got back when I needed to leave this morning, so I was stuck with his old banger."

"Yeah, we believe you," Jack grinned.

Alan led them to the locker room where they could safely leave their valuables, then they headed to the first tee. It was good to be out early and the first group on the course. The sun was already beginning to take on some heat and a faint mist was rising from around the flag on the green they were aiming for.

They played the first few holes amid a lot of good-natured banter as they caught up with each other's news. The seventh was situated near to a small copse of beech trees, and Jack hit a brilliant shot onto the green, just short of the hole. Fred followed with a ball which fell quite a few yards short, while Mark's was right off course and flew past into the bunker, earning him a few ribald comments and some mock sympathy. Alan's shot landed on the edge of the green so he lifted the flag for Jack to tap his ball in for a birdie. It still took Alan two putts to sink his, and just as he was bending to retrieve it there was a shout from Mark who was running back towards them from the bunker.

"There's a woman in there!" he yelled. " I think she's dead!"

Fred, who had a first aid certificate, took the lead and jogged past them to look into the sand trap. The others followed but kept their distance. Even before he checked for a pulse, it was obvious that he wasn't going to find one.

Alan took over command. "Fred, can you phone the police and explain what we've found?"

"Of course." He took out his phone while Alan called the clubhouse to ensure any newcomers weren't allowed on the course.

"Stay on the green, everyone. I assume the police will want to speak to all of us. I'll go back and waylay anyone already on the course."

He rushed off back along the route they had taken.

CHAPTER 3

Saturday 8th October

DCI Ben Cooke was whistling happily as he finished loading the dishwasher. Alice had left straight after breakfast to make the finishing touches to the flower arrangements at the church in readiness for a wedding this afternoon, so the morning was his to waste. The sun was up and it was good to leave the car at home and take Buster for a walk through the park to the newsagent. It seemed that he wasn't the only one who had been lured outdoors by the sunshine as there were many others enjoying a stroll; some hand-in-hand with a partner, some on their own, others like himself, with a canine friend or two, but all smiling and sauntering along without a care in the world.

On his return he slipped a pod into the coffee machine with a view to taking his paper into the garden and top up his vitamin D while he read all the local news. He hadn't got past the front page before his mobile began to ring. Seeing the station's number, he sighed; so much for his quiet weekend off.

"DCI Cooke," he said with a sad lack of enthusiasm.

"Sir, we have a situation at the Wellsend Golf Course. Some lads have found a body."

"I'll be there in fifteen minutes."

He swigged down the rest of his coffee as he went indoors, found an old envelope and scribbled a message for Alice. Leaving Buster curled up in his bed, he took his keys from the hook and set off.

Wellsend was a members-only club laid out on the escarpment above the town. Not a fan of the sport, Cooke had only been there once, a couple of years ago, to a fundraising event which the Commissioner had organised. It hadn't been his idea of a good night out, dressed up in a monkey suit and hobnobbing with the elite, but it was a necessary evil. The clubhouse, a modern building constructed of local stone, was well in keeping with its setting and hidden from view from the main road, and he had to slow down to look out for the sign at the end of the track which led to it.

There were about a dozen vehicles in the car park, including the patrol car with PC Milner leaning against its bonnet, his face turned towards the sun. Hearing his superior's footsteps approaching he quickly levered himself up and came to meet him.

"Morning sir. The body is quite a walk from here – at the seventh hole. We've set up the police tape and Truman is talking to the lads who found her. Forensics are on their way."

Cooke looked around at the cars. "Are there still players on the course?"

"There were a couple of groups who had already started playing and were sent back to the clubhouse. I've had a word with them and none of them had noticed anything out of the ordinary. I've taken their details and no one else is being allowed on."

"Anyone else here?"

"Just the guy in the shop and the catering staff in the clubhouse."

Cooke started to walk towards the course and Milner fell into step with him.

"So what do we know?"

"Woman, early to mid forties. Four lads found her in the bunker at about 9.30. They were first on the course this morning."

"Is there any identification on the body?"

"There was no handbag, and one shoe is missing."

"Who's the pathologist?"

"It's Bellingham. Not a happy man as he was already on his way here to play when he got the call."

As they neared the scene, Cooke could see three of the lads sitting on the grass outside the blue and white tape with their backs to the bunker where Bellingham was already inspecting the body, while the fourth was nearby talking to PC Truman. He stopped to put on plastic shoe covers before lifting the tape and approaching the short rotund figure of the pathologist.

"So?"

"Good morning to you too," Bellingham replied.

Cooke looked past him to the young woman, face down, fully clothed in skimpy black dress and short red jacket, her shoulder-length blonde hair caked in sand and blood. "What can you tell me?"

Bellingham pointed out the obvious. "There is evidence of a blow to the head."

"Time of death?"

"Give me chance. Can you help me turn her over?"

After a swift visual examination Bellingham closed the eyelids over the vacant blue eyes.

"Look at these marks on her neck."

Cooke looked, and then studied the ground around the body. "No sign of a struggle. Almost certainly not where she was killed. Any idea on time?"

Bellingham looked at his thermometer.

"I would say somewhere around midnight. I'll send through a preliminary report once I've got her back to my lair." He bent a little closer. "There's something in her pocket." He pulled out a set of keys.

Cooke took out a plastic bag and Bellingham dropped in a Peugeot fob with another couple of keys attached to it.

"I'll leave you to get on with your work. Let me

know when the post mortem is."

"Will do."

Cooke walked towards the lads and showed his ID. "DCI Cooke. Any of you know the deceased? Was she a member?"

Alan made the introductions, explaining that he helped run the shop and also gave private golf lessons; he had never seen her at the club. The other three were his friends, who had travelled from different parts of the country this morning.

"Is the course locked up at night?" Cooke asked him.

"Nobody can play in the dark, so it hardly seems necessary," Alan shrugged.

"Which one of you found her?"

"Mark. He's over there, talking to your man; he's pretty shook up."

"Has anyone touched the body?"

Fred raised a hand. "I'm a first-aider so I went to see if there was anything I could do, but it was obvious that she was dead before I felt for a pulse. I didn't touch her otherwise."

Cooke handed Alan his card. "If you hear anything from any of the members or think of anything that might have struck you as odd recently give me a ring."

Truman was just finishing his conversation with Mark and was thanking him for his help when Cooke reached him. Mark left to join his mates and the constable turned his attention to his superior.

"Good morning, sir. Mr Hanley there has just described how he found the body but didn't have anything else to add. Do you want us to talk to anyone else?"

"No, just make sure you get contact details for the other three lads. It doesn't sound as if she was a member – although her assailant may be. I need you both to stay here until the PCSO arrives to take over, then I want you both back at the station with a full report."

Cooke made his way over to one of the white-clad figures who had arrived in the meantime and was taking photos a short distance away.

The man looked up as Cooke approached holding out his warrant card.

"DCI Cooke. What have you got there?"

"The buckle is broken," the man replied, pointing at a scratched red sandal near his feet. "Not the best footwear for running, although she may have caught it if she climbed over that wall. There's a couple of toppers been dislodged."

Cooke looked towards the wall and saw where it had lost a couple of stones, and noticed a camper van driving past.

"That's the main Chesterfield road, isn't it?"

"Yes, but there is no vehicle access to the course from that side."

"So where was he parked?" Cooke pondered. "I'll drive along there and have a look."

As he walked back to his car, he thought about going into the clubhouse but decided against it for the moment. He drove a short way along the main road before he found a lay-by just past where the forensic team had been working on the other side of the wall. He pulled in, crossed the road and walked back along the narrow grass verge to where he could shout to the man he had spoken to earlier.

"There's a lay-by about fifty yards up. It might be useful to give that a looking at when you've finished there."

"Okay."

CHAPTER 4

Sunday 9th October

Cooke had stayed on to set up the white board last night once he'd read the constable's report, but still arrived early at the station this morning and was pleased to find the preliminary report from Bellingham waiting on his desk. He read it, making a note of the important details, and noted that the post-mortem would be on Monday at 2pm.

He picked up Truman's account and re-read it, but there was nothing helpful there. It might be worth having a more detailed chat with Alan Williams later since he worked at the golf club.

He walked down to the main office to find those members of his team scheduled to work this morning and approached DS Wendy Robins' desk. She was busy at her keyboard but looked up when he drew near.

"Good morning, sir."

"Good morning, Wendy. Do we have a name yet for our victim?"

"I've checked, sir, and no missing persons have been reported locally."

"It might be a bit early. People seem to think they have to wait at least a day before reporting someone missing. It's possible she's not local so get onto the NCA, spread the search wider."

A meeting on the case had been called for 11am and all the team had been notified. Cooke returned to the office he shared with DI Sharon Whittaker, who was away this weekend attending her niece's Christening and would be back tomorrow. He pulled a new manila folder from the small stationery cupboard and slotted in the reports before writing the crime reference on the front.

Cooke's stomach was complaining about the lack of breakfast, and with some time yet until the meeting he strolled down to Lettuce Eat in search of sustenance.

The Indian summer continued, and Cooke enjoyed his bacon and brie ciabatta sandwich on a bench in the dappled shade of a large oak tree outside the station before returning to start the briefing.

He looked round the room and was pleased to see that everyone was punctual.

"Okay, folks. We have the body of a woman, early to mid forties, found by some young players at Wellsend Golf Course yesterday morning. So far we don't have a name. One of the lads is the club professional and he said he didn't recognise her. The others are his mates who had arrived bright and early from other parts of the country.

"Although there were marks on her neck, the

hyoid bone wasn't fractured, and it looks like her death was due to a blow she had sustained to the side of the head. Time of death between eleven thirty pm and one am. Bloods have been sent off so we will soon know whether she was drunk or drugged at all."

"Some keys found in the victim's pocket," he held up the bag. "There's a Yale, and a very small one which may be for a padlock or suitcase, both attached to a Peugeot key fob. We know the vehicle's not in the club car park, so where is it? "

"She might have broken down some distance away and been trying to walk home," suggested Tom.

"Or she travelled with her assailant," added Jimmy.

"If she had walked it can't have been far in the sandals she was wearing, as her feet didn't look damaged. It might be worth looking more closely in the local area."

He was interrupted by a knock at the door, and one of the clerical staff entered and handed him a sheet of paper.

He read it before walking over to the wall behind him and pointing at a large-scale map of the golf club and its surroundings.

"Because her missing sandal was found on the grass nearby it was originally thought she might have broken the buckle climbing the wall on the side of the main road here, as she tried to escape her assailant." He tapped the page he was holding.

"They have now found a large blood-stained stone between the seventh hole and a small copse just here. A sample has been sent to the lab to check if it's a match to that of our victim."

He studied the map.

"A footpath runs through the golf course here," he pointed, "and skirts the edge of the copse to an exit onto the main road here. Truman, you and Hughes drive up there and see if there is anywhere near this exit where a car could park up. There are some cottages nearby on the main road. Go and have a word with the occupants, see if they saw or heard anything. Keep a look out for the Peugeot while you're up there."

"Yes, sir."

"Anything from NCA, Wendy?"

"No, sir, but I've given them a description from your notes."

Tom Golding raised his hand.

"Jacobs has been on the blower sniffing for information. I told him I'd get back to him."

The local reporter had eyes and ears everywhere and had already contacted Cooke on Saturday when he'd got wind of the death at the golf club. All he'd been able to tell him then was that a body had been found.

"Tell him we're looking for information from anyone who may have been in the area on Friday night to get in touch if they saw anything which might help in our enquiries.

"Someone must have missed her by now. The

sooner we get a name, the sooner we can solve this. Okay everyone. Same time tomorrow."

Amanda was in the back garden planting a few late pansies, the first she had grown herself from seed, when she heard the back gate creak open, and looked up.

"Hello, Mum," Lauren greeted her. "I tried the front door and realised you must be out here."

"Hello, Lauren, love. Put the kettle on, would you? I've just a couple left to do and I'll be finished."

Amanda was always pleased to see her daughter, who often popped in to see her and keep an eye on her since losing her dad.

With the last plant firmed in and watered, Amanda picked up her bits and pieces and put them by the shed door just as Lauren placed two mugs of coffee onto the blue metal garden table.

"How was your day with your friend yesterday?" Lauren asked.

"I didn't see her," she said with a shrug as she settled onto one of the chairs.

"Oh - that's a shame. What was the problem?"

"She didn't turn up."

"Didn't turn up as in just didn't arrive?"

"I waited over two hours in Stow square and I don't know whether to be worried or annoyed. I sent her several texts when she was late but I haven't heard anything back. I'm beginning to wonder if she ever intended to come. I tried ringing again last night but there was no answer, and I just don't know what to think."

"I do hope everything is okay with her and you hear from her soon but..."

"But what?"

"Well, how well do you really know her? You only met earlier this year."

"I know, but we spent a lot of time together and liked the same things. It seemed like we'd known each other for much longer."

CHAPTER 5

Monday 10th October

Cooke had never felt the least desire to join the realms of social media. He didn't need to see the self-absorbed nonsense that so many seemed to post – where they were eating that burger and chips, or birthday wishes to a child who was too young to read let alone have an account – but he'd heard his colleagues moaning about it often enough.

However, he could see that it could be a useful tool. Just last week his neighbour's dog had been reunited with its owners after their message had been read by others far and wide. Today he was prepared to praise its virtues as, after Jacobs had posted his update on the newspaper's Facebook page, several calls had come through with information. Jimmy had offered to visit the Duck and Drake last night to follow up three different sightings of a woman who may have been the victim.

Cooke had taken a call from a Danny Cavendish, who said he had nearly been taken out by another driver on Friday night on the road about half a mile from the golf course. He was returning from a night out with his mates when a car slewed at speed round the bend ahead of him and was heading straight for him, almost losing control before speeding past and missing him by a whisker. It had all happened so quickly that he couldn't say what make of car it was, but that it was a medium sized saloon, and his headlights had illuminated a metallic silver flank as it shot past.

There were plenty of silver cars on the road, but this could be the first piece in the jigsaw.

Cooke was busy trying to clear some of the mountain of paperwork in his in-tray when Sharon appeared clutching two takeaway coffee cups. She placed one on his desk.

"Thanks, just what I needed. Good weekend?"

"Yeah. Good to see everyone, and little Elsa was adorable."

He brought her up to date on the case so far while they drank their coffee.

"Let's go and see how the team are getting on."

All eyes were on Cooke as he strode into the main open-plan office, and the hubbub of noise ceased as if a switch had been thrown. Everyone waiting to hear what the boss had to say, but it wasn't much.

"We still haven't got a lot to go on. One of the cottages nearby is empty and the occupants of the other are both sound sleepers and didn't hear a thing. Forensics are still on site, but as yet they've found nothing more of any significance."

"We've had a few bites from the report on Facebook," Golding said. "I've a couple more leads to follow up."

"Could be helpful," Cooke nodded. "A speeding silver car was seen in the vicinity at around the right time, according to someone I have just spoken to. Any luck with the CCTV you got from the Duck and Drake, Jimmy?"

"I've looked through it but it doesn't look like our woman – too young."

"I need you to follow up any other sightings – especially the ones with a man."

He noticed Wendy trying to come in discreetly and raised one eyebrow.

"Sorry I'm late, sir. I've just returned a phone call which could be of interest."

"I'm all ears."

"The caller was a Mrs Linda Watson, 23 Skylark Drive, Ashthorp. She and her husband arrived back home from foreign climes on Saturday evening. They had left their home in the capable hands of a house and pet-sitter who had been recommended by a friend. On their return they were surprised to see the woman's car on their drive, and on entering the house found that her things were still in the spare room. This was odd because she'd said she would feed the animals on Saturday morning and leave straight afterwards. She still hasn't appeared."

"What make of car?" Tom Golding asked.

"A Peugeot 108."

"Did you get the registration?"

"She was ringing from work and hadn't thought to write it down."

Cooke took the piece of notepaper that Wendy was holding and showed it to Sharon before handing it back.

"Wendy, go and speak to the neighbours see what they can tell us about the house-sitter - her comings and goings, and whether they'd spoken to her. Take a note of her car registration and find out who it's registered to. I've got the post mortem to attend this afternoon. Sharon, you and I will go and visit the Watsons this evening. Tom, is Jacobs doing a piece for tonight's Herald?"

"Yes, sir."

"A lot of people won't have seen it online so hopefully we can jog some memories. We need to stress that this is a suspicious death so encourage him to get it in a prominent position – preferably on the front page. I'll leave it to you to phone him."

"Anything else?"

No-one spoke.

"Okay, any developments, let me know."

PMs were always grim, and when Cooke left Bellingham he headed straight for the park. He needed fresh air to get the smell and taste out of his system. After wandering past flower beds, now empty and ready to be replenished with winter flowering plants, he sat on a bench to think about what had been revealed. The knock on the head had been the cause of death, which had been narrowed down now to the earlier part of the time window; the blood on the stone had matched that of the victim, and stomach contents had shown up nothing other than crisps, cola and chocolate cake – no traces of drugs or alcohol. The picture was beginning to be filled in, piece by piece.

CHAPTER 6

Monday 10th October

Although it was still warm in the daytime it was starting to get chilly by evening and Cooke found Sharon waiting for him with her jacket on.

Cooke picked up his mobile phone and car keys and they walked together to the car park at the back of the building.

"Do you know what part of Ashthorp we're heading for?" he asked as they pulled out onto the road.

"Yes, it's on the new development near the light industrial estate."

The small cul-de-sac, a mixture of modern red-brick detached and semi-detached houses, was easily found. As Cooke drove Sharon squinted to read the numbers on the doors. Each house was set behind a neatly mown lawn with a narrow flower border where it met the pavement.

Sharon counted the odd numbers on the left-hand side. "There it is." She pointed at the next house along where a White Kia was parked behind a small purple Peugeot.

Cooke indicated and pulled up next to the kerb just past the drive, released his seatbelt and noticed a curtain move in a window opposite as he opened the car door.

"The neighbourhood watch has clocked us," he said, jerking his head to indicate the window.

"Useful to have a few nosey neighbours. Let's hope Wendy had some luck speaking to them."

They walked up the drive and past a small window to the white UPVC front door. Sharon admired the kingfisher depicted in its round coloured-glass window as Cooke rapped on the knocker.

A man in his early thirties came to the door wearing an open neck white shirt and smart tailored trousers. After introducing themselves and showing warrants they were invited inside and shown into a bright and airy room to the right, with a large window looking out onto the front lawn.

"Take a seat. Linda won't be long. Would you like a drink? We were just going to open a bottle of wine."

"No, thank you, sir, not while we're on duty. But please, go ahead, by all means."

"I'll go and get Linda," Oliver Watson said as he left the room.

Sharon sat on the comfortable fabric sofa taking out her notepad and pen while Cooke wandered around the neat living room, taking in the Swedish design furniture, a vase of bright mixed gerberas, and a collage of wedding photos. He was having a better look at a piece of artwork on the wall above a mock fireplace housing an electric fire when the couple joined them.

"Are you sure you don't want to join us?" Linda raised her glass of chilled white wine as she sat in an armchair, her husband perching on the arm.

"No, thank you." Cooke sat next to Sharon.

"Could you tell me when you arrived home and found your house-sitter missing?" he asked.

After a quick glance at Linda, Oliver took the lead.

"We got home about nine o'clock on Saturday evening and were surprised to see her car on the drive. She'd said she wanted to leave early on Saturday as she had a long journey to make for an appointment later that morning, so would go after feeding the animals."

"Was the door locked when you arrived?"

"Yes, and the house was in darkness. I remember having to unlock the back door, and I heard Milo – that's our cat – crying on the kitchen windowsill. He rushed in straight to his empty food bowl. Poor thing was starving and wolfed his food down."

"When did you leave for your holiday?"

"Last Saturday. Mrs Lawrence arrived here on the Friday evening to get settled in."

"How did you find your house sitter?"

"I was telling a work colleague that I really wanted to take Linda away but I was worried because although I'm sure one of the neighbours would nip round and feed the cat and rabbits, with all the recent burglaries I didn't want to leave the house empty."

Linda took over. "We haven't been away for some years because of the animals. They're my babies and I couldn't bear to think of leaving them again after the last time. Mrs Green from up the road offered to feed them. Ray, the old boy from next door told me she'd left my bunnies in the run all week. They were really poorly when we got back - it had rained here most of the time we were away."

"No wonder the hutch was so clean," Oliver added.

"Do you have an address for Mrs Lawrence?"

"No, we contacted her on the mobile phone number that Chris gave me. Oh, wait a minute – she gave you a business card, didn't she, Linda?"

"Yes, now where did I put it?" She put her glass down and went off to look for it.

"Perhaps we could see the room she slept in while she was here," Cooke suggested.

"Of course. We haven't touched anything."

Cooke and Sharon followed him to the room on the first floor.

"I'll leave you to it," Oliver said as he opened the door for them.

After putting on gloves, Cooke followed Sharon into the spacious room, decorated in warm shades of ochre and yellow. A small suitcase sat on the neatly made bed, packed but left open for the last few items. On the chest of drawers a laptop computer was plugged in but turned off at the socket.

"We'll get Jimmy to look at this," Sharon said.

Cooke looked up from his position at the bedside cabinet, where next to the lamp a small digital alarm clock informed them that it was 18.00 and nodded.

He picked up a hard back book entitled *Steamy Nights in Tuscany* with a cover picture of an undulating landscape of cypress trees leading to a distant dwelling; a bookmark was inserted at the beginning of Chapter Three. He looked inside the front of the book and found that it had been signed by the author.

"Ever heard of Jason Partridge?" Cooke asked as he showed her the signature.

"No, can't say that I have. Doesn't look like the sort of thing I'd want to read."

Sharon opened both of the smaller drawers in the unit and found clean underwear in one and socks and a small jewellery box in the other. She flipped the lid of the box to find a white gold wedding band. "Look at this. I wonder why she wasn't wearing it."

"She was wearing a ring on her wedding finger, but it was more like a figure of eight on its side."

"Sounds like an infinity ring – a sort of friendship ring. Maybe she had a lover."

In the small drawer of the bedside cabinet

Cooke found a cosmetic bag and a packet of contraceptive pills.

Sharon unplugged the laptop and gave it to Cooke, who balanced the book on top of it. She picked up the ring box and they went downstairs to find the Watsons sitting on stools near the French windows which opened onto the back garden, where a couple of well-fed rabbits were enjoying the freedom of their run on the lawn.

"We're taking these with us." Sharon indicated the items with a small wave of her hand. "I'll go and fetch a receipt book from the car."

"We'll arrange to pick up the car tomorrow but we'll leave the rest of her belongings for a few days more in case she returns in the meantime," Cooke told them even though he was pretty sure that she wouldn't. "If anyone else turns up asking to take anything, please contact us."

Sharon came back and gave a slip of paper to Linda who picked up a small card from the worktop nearby and gave it to her in return. "That's the one she left with us, with all her contact details."

"Thanks, that's really helpful."

As they left Sharon glanced at the card and found that the name and address agreed with the vehicle registration details Wendy had phoned through earlier. They had already ascertained that Mrs Lawrence was married and the latest electoral roll had recorded a Charles Lawrence living at the same address near Bath in Somerset. She would need to contact the local force who could inform her husband and ask him if he would come and identify her body.

CHAPTER 7

Tuesday 11th October

Cooke found typed notes from Wendy on his desk when he arrived next morning. She hadn't been able to track down many of the Watsons' neighbours. Most of those she had managed to speak to had seen Valerie Lawrence during the week, either walking or driving past, and one or two had spoken to her about the weather or just to say hello in passing. Wendy had left a written note at the bottom saying that she would go back in the evening when she thought she had more chance of finding people at home.

He phoned through to the station mechanic asking him to collect the Peugeot from the Watsons' driveway, then, restless, he rose and walked over to the window. The once lush green leaves of the oak, which had obscured his view all summer, were looking jaded in the early October sunlight and it wouldn't be long before they turned to copper brown and fell. He liked the colours of autumn but hated the thought of the cold winter's days and nights that followed.

Last night he hadn't slept well, probably due to eating late and finishing up the stilton, so when he had finally dozed off it was into a deep sleep, only to wake thick-headed at the sound of the alarm. Some serious caffeine was required to kick-start his brain, and not the foul excuse from the vending machine, so he took a walk round the corner and got himself a decent cup from Brian's Den.

The fresh air was a tonic in itself, and he found Brian in good spirits. Cooke returned nursing one of the new reusable coffee cups, which Brian was promoting, and a white paper bag containing a sausage roll which had arrived fresh out of the oven while he was chatting and could not be resisted.

As he entered the car park Sharon was driving out, and she wound down her window.

"Can't stop, I'm meeting Charles Lawrence at the morgue, and I'm hoping to have a quick chat with him after he's identified his wife's body."

"Can't he come here afterwards?"

"No. He's got to rush off to Peterborough as he has a eulogy to read at an old friend's funeral at 3pm this afternoon."

"Poor bugger. What a day he must be having."

Cooke had no sooner sat down and was about to take a bite of his pastry treat when there was a knock at the door and Wendy stuck her head in.

"Come and sit down. Did you have better luck last night?"

"A lot of the same, but the woman across the road at number eighteen said one evening the lady in question was picked up by a silver Toyota, and she was sure it was a man driving. She remembered it was Friday evening because she was getting her bins in. Says he was quite tall but not six foot, casually dressed, and had short wavy hair, but she didn't actually see his face."

"Praise be to curtain twitchers! I don't suppose she got the registration? "

"Unfortunately not. She knew that the number was sixty - her age apparently - but couldn't remember any of the letters apart from the fact that the last three spelt out a word."

Glen Jeffries spent most of his working days driving around in his council pick-up truck emptying litter bins. Yesterday had been heavy work after the weekend and although on the whole he enjoyed his job, he was looking forward to retiring in a couple of years' time. Today wasn't his favourite day of the week because it was dog bin day. It took him out into the smaller villages and the more obscure places in the district, where footpaths and bridleways brought folk out to enjoy the beautiful countryside with their canine friends, and many, though by no means all, of them wanted somewhere to dispose of their poo-laden plastic bags. Unfortunately for him, not everyone closed the bag securely and the smell was disgusting when he came to empty them out.

With an early start, Glen had covered quite a bit of ground and had emptied a dozen or so bins, tying the top of each bag then hurling it into the back of his pick-up truck before inserting a clean black sack. The sun had broken through as he had driven up the main road out of Wellsend and he knew that a treat awaited him at his next stop, where he usually took his lunch break on a Tuesday. He reversed his truck a few yards into the wide entrance of a bridleway from where he could see beech trees on one side and a magnificent view on the other. He sat watching a couple of red kites soaring gracefully above before grabbing a wet wipe from the packet he kept close at all times – you never knew when you would need one – and wiped his hands thoroughly before opening his lunch box and taking out a scotch egg. He took a gulp of ice-cold squash from his special flask and with the window open, listened to the different birds singing in the trees all around.

There was a lot more ground to cover, so reluctantly he put his lunch box and flask neatly on the passenger seat and walked over to the lidded metal bin which was attached to a telegraph pole. He was just about to bunch up the plastic and tie a knot in the top of the bag when he noticed something red and shiny inside. It would be a good idea to put on some latex gloves which, although supplied by the council, he rarely used as he didn't like the smell they left on his hands. Today the thought of actually putting his bare hand into this sack was enough to make it necessary. He pushed a neatly tied small green bag out of the way and pulled out a red patent clutch bag. It reminded him of the news item in last night's Herald, and realising he wasn't far from where the body had been found, he thought it was possible this might be evidence. He tied the sack and threw it into the back of the truck then put the handbag carefully in the passenger foot well. Only then did he remove his gloves, and although he hadn't actually touched anything nasty, thoroughly cleaned his hands again before reaching for his phone to ring his wife.

"Freda, can you get last night's paper? I need you to look at something for me."

He waited and when she came back to the phone asked, "On the front page. What was the crime number and phone number to call in the article about the dead woman?"

He already had pen and paper ready and jotted the information down as she relayed it to him.

"Thanks, dear. I think I might have found something for them," he told her before hanging up and dialling the number he'd just been given.

DS Tom Golding had been taking phone calls on the incident line this morning with possible sightings of Valerie. He'd logged them all, with the caller's name and phone number, taking down as good a description of anyone accompanying her as he could get from each caller and thanking them for their help. He wasn't feeling very hopeful, so when the phone rang at 10.30 he sighed before picking up. His interest was soon piqued as the caller told him about the handbag he had found not far from the golf course. Eager to get it back to the station, Golding arranged for a squad car to go and collect it from the man, and ran up to let Cooke know, almost bumping into him as he turned the corner at the top of the stairs.

"I was just coming to see how Jimmy was getting on with the laptop, but the handbag could hold really useful information," Cooke said as they walked down together. They found Jimmy with the laptop open on the desk in front of him but the man himself stuffing the remainder of a doughnut into his mouth, not quickly enough to prevent a big splodge of jam ending up on the front of his shirt.

Cooke scowled at him. "What have you found so far?"

Jimmy rubbed his hands together, ineffectively trying to rid them of sugar.

"Mainly items related to her pet and house-sitting job. Recent search history seems to be related to local restaurants and pubs. She'd been shopping at Amazon and looking at a holiday company website. No log-ins to Facebook or Twitter, but she might do that on her mobile if she has either account. I'll look at her photo files next."

"Keep looking – and for heaven's sake wash your hands." Turning to Golding, he said, "Let me know as soon as that bag gets here."

CHAPTER 8

Tuesday 11th October

The bag, when it arrived, revealed only a few items; a driving licence, a mobile phone, and a small purse containing a debit card, two ten pound notes and some loose change. Cooke picked up the driving licence.

"Valerie Fiona Lawrence, born twenty sixth of June, 1977. That would make her forty five. Tom, send a copy of the photo to Jacobs. It may well help jog some memories."

Cooke then gave the mobile to Jimmy to work his magic on and was hoping that as well as any recent calls it would contain more of her online activity, in particular any social media posts she may have made recently.

Sharon arrived back from the mortuary while Cooke was talking to Jimmy.

"How did it go?" he asked.

"He seemed pretty stoic when he entered the viewing room, but broke down as soon as he saw his wife. He whispered something to her, sobbing and holding her hand. Then suddenly, as if he remembered there was someone else present, he stood up, gently replaced her hand and walked out. I followed and offered him a coffee, and we went to sit in the little anteroom.

"He told me she had been looking after her mother, who needed help on her discharge from hospital after an operation. The last time they'd spoken was on Friday evening - she always phoned him at around the same time. They'd had words but he had still expected her home Saturday afternoon and was concerned when she hadn't arrived or phoned by 7pm so tried her mobile, but it was switched off. After another hour he finally rang his mother-in-law, but she didn't pick up. He hadn't known what to think, but decided the old girl may have needed to go back to hospital and that would have explained why his wife's phone was turned off."

"Didn't he try calling her again when she didn't arrive home on Sunday?"

"He said he'd intended to but his phone network was down most of the day, although he did leave a curt message Sunday evening when it was up and running again and he hadn't found any missed calls or messages from her. Apparently when they last spoke on Friday, she told him she'd accepted a house-sitting job starting on the Sunday, and he hadn't been best pleased as she had been away a week already. He thought she'd still got the hump with him and gone straight there."

"If she usually rang him every day, surely he

would have expected to hear from her on Monday, once she'd had time to cool down, especially as he'd left a message."

"He had to go into the office early Monday morning for a meeting and was rather more annoyed with her than worried. I didn't have time to ask anything else because he was eager to leave, and as he had calmed down and seemed safe enough to drive, I couldn't really keep him any longer."

"First impressions?"

"He seemed genuinely upset, and if it was him who killed her, I don't think it was pre-meditated."

"A pity he couldn't stay a bit longer, but with that distance to travel it's obvious he couldn't."

"He said he would be at home from late tomorrow, and I've got his number if you would like to speak to him."

"I think I'd rather go down there to see him face to face. Can you arrange that for Thursday?"

"Will do, guv."

Armed with the driving licence, Jimmy had been able to open the phone quite quickly. He never could understand why people weren't more sensible when choosing a password. She had used her middle name, Fiona, plus the date and month of her birthday, 2606. He gathered his scribbled notes and went up to discuss his findings with Cooke and Sharon.

"She doesn't seem to have any social media

accounts and has very few people listed in her contacts. There is an interesting voice mail left from someone called Amanda on Saturday who was obviously expecting to meet her, and a different woman left an irate message on Sunday when Valerie hadn't arrived – I've made a note of the phone numbers for you. One missed call and a message from Charles. Other than that there were several phone calls to and from an unregistered mobile. The last registered owner sold it, complete with sim card, on Marketplace over a year ago. Apart from Charles, her contacts only consisted of plumber, doctor, etcetera. Internet history was mainly businesses in the area local to where she was staying, restaurants, shops and a Peugeot garage. Her photo files were just views or buildings – not a person among them."

"That unregistered mobile would have been useful. Is it possible to trace the owner?"

"I've tried, but it's switched off at the moment. I'll keep trying."

"The angry woman will be the person she had arranged to house-sit for. I'll give her number a try; someone needs to tell her why her sitter didn't turn up. Sharon, give the Saturday woman a call, see what you can find out about their scheduled meeting. Anything else, Jimmy?"

"Her calendar had blocks of dates highlighted with a name and phone number and at least a couple of dates within each block marked with an asterisk."

"I wonder what those were. Call the first couple and see what you can find out. Can you print the calendar off for me? I'll ask her husband if he knows. There might be a physical diary at her home."

Jimmy delivered the printout after he had spoken to a Mrs Wright, who was expecting Valerie Lawrence to look after her house and three cats for a week at the end of November. She didn't know why a couple of dates had been marked with an asterisk as they didn't correspond with bin day.

Jacobs had wasted no time in securing a slot on the front page of this evening's Riversmeet Herald. Now able to use a photo of the murdered woman, he had written out his report, containing as much information as the police had given him and ending with the details of how the public could help them with their investigation along with the case number to quote. His report would be seen by the many readers of the popular local paper.

One of those readers, Sid Davies, picked up his copy from the doormat and took it through to the kitchen where his wife was putting the finishing touches to their evening meal. He sat at the ready-laid table to quickly scan the back page and catch up on all the local sports news until his wife placed his dinner in front of him, and he folded the paper in half and set it down beside his plate. His wife sat down opposite and started to tell him about the new ladies' club she had attended that afternoon when she stopped mid-sentence.

"Sid! That looks like the Merry Widow."

She was pointing at the photo on the front of the newspaper. Sid picked it up and his wife looked on as he read out loud.

"Woman found murdered at local Golf Course."

He looked at the photo. "It does look a bit like her. What was her name?"

"I don't know, I never actually spoke to her, although she always joined the rest of us in the bar after dinner. Not a shrinking violet, that's for sure."

"That's why you called her the Merry Widow. I seem to remember she said she was from Gloucestershire."

"Perhaps we ought to call the police."

"We haven't got anything useful to tell them, we'd just be wasting their time."

"I could tell them about how she kept us awake that night in Florence entertaining some man friend in her room. Came down to breakfast the next morning all prim and proper as if butter wouldn't melt."

"I hardly think that will be of much help to them. She was a free agent and it was none of our business."

Sid put the paper down and carried on eating his meal.

CHAPTER 9

Wednesday 12th October

Sharon had tried phoning Amanda Hanks numerous times with no success but decided to give it one more try before knocking off for the day. She was about to give up when a breathless voice answered.

"Hello?"

"Good evening. Am I speaking to Amanda Hanks?"

"Yes," was the wary reply.

"This is DI Sharon Whittaker of Riversmeet police in Derbyshire."

"Did you say you were from Derbyshire?"

"Yes."

"But I'm in Gloucestershire and I don't know anyone in Derbyshire, so I don't understand why you would be ringing me."

"Let me explain. I believe you know Valerie Lawrence? We found your messages on her mobile phone and it sounds like you were expecting to meet her."

"That's right, we agreed to meet in Stow on

the Wold, just up the road from me, on Saturday morning and she was going to visit relations in Chipping Norton afterwards. I waited for a couple of hours but she didn't show up."

"There's no easy way to say this, but I'm sorry to tell you that your friend died the day before she was due to meet you."

"But she was so healthy – the life and soul of the party. Was it an accident?"

"It looks like she may have been murdered."

"Oh no! She was my friend." Amanda sniffed to hold back the tears.

"We're trying to find out more about her, and hoped that you may be able to help. How long have you been friends?"

"Well, I only met her back in May when we were on the same holiday to Italy. She'd been allotted the seat next to me on the coach and we hit it off straight away. She's a widow, like me, and we got on so well we've kept in touch ever since."

"Widow, you say?"

"Yes, he must have had a good job because he left her quite well off."

Sharon was beginning to wonder how well Amanda really knew the person she called her friend.

"So you would be surprised to hear that we've been talking to Valerie's husband?"

"Very. She told us she was a widow."

Sharon made a note and carried on.

"Which holiday company did you travel with?"

"Tour2Explore Holidays."

"And you say you went to Italy?"

"Yes. We had a wonderful time and visited Pisa, Florence, Rome and Sorrento before ending up at Lake Garda. We found we liked the same things and enjoyed walking around the different cities together."

"Did the two of you make any other friends on the trip?"

"Oh yes, there were six of us, all single travellers who seemed to gravitate to the same table on the first night, and ate together for the whole fortnight. We called ourselves 'The Single Six'."

"Who were the others?"

"Well, there was Valerie and me," Sharon could imagine Amanda counting the others on her fingers as she spoke, "and Mary – she was a retired schoolteacher who had us in stitches with some of the stories she told about the things the children said and did. Then there was Adrian, a young student doing history or art, I can't remember, and he was as camp as could be and a bit on the quiet side. Whenever we saw him out and about, he was taking photos. Giles – sorry, I've no idea what he did for a living. I think he was sweet on Valerie, as he always made sure he sat next to her at dinner. That's five, and lastly Steve, a real down to earth character who seemed to like golf as he often went to Spain on golfing holidays."

"What date in May did you go?"

"I'll just go and check my calendar for the exact dates."

Sharon could hear her running upstairs, doodling on her pad as she waited, and had completed a skeletal tree by the time Amanda returned.

"May 7th to the 21st."

"Do you think she said she was a widow because you are?"

"She didn't know. I have to be honest, I told a fib too - I told them I was married, although poor Geoffrey died two years ago. Lauren, that's my daughter, told me to pretend to be married so that I didn't get any of the wrong attention from any single males on the trip. It was quite handy actually as I'm not a big drinker and I was able to go to my room after dinner, saying I was ringing home, and I could actually enjoy reading my book while a lot of the others went to the bar."

"Did Valerie go to her room too?"

"As far as I know. She always took the lift with me after dinner. At some hotels we were on the same floor so we'd walk together to whoever's room was first or say goodnight in the lift if we were on different floors."

"Thank you for your time, Mrs Hanks."

"Sorry I haven't been much help."

"You have been most helpful." Sharon replied as she hung up.

It was interesting that Valerie had pretended to be a widow. Was she looking for a holiday romance or was she just using the white lie to befriend Amanda? Either way, she didn't feel any nearer to knowing what Valerie Lawrence was like as a person.

CHAPTER 10

Thursday 13th October

Bath was on Alice Cooke's bucket list of places she wanted to visit so she didn't need asking twice. It just took a quick phone call to her friend, a keen rambler, who was happy to have Buster for the day, and she was free to accompany her husband.

Having dropped off their beloved cocker spaniel where he would be well looked after and given a good walk, Ben and Alice were enjoying the Derbyshire countryside as they headed towards the M1 and the drive south.

"There's so much to see that I won't manage it all in one day," Alice told Cooke. "There's the Roman Baths, the Costume Museum, the Abbey, the Jane Austen Centre, and I've got to try a Bath Bun."

"You can get me one while you're at it."

"I read there's an open topped bus ride that I can take so I can hop on and off and enjoy the commentary in between."

"Leave the baths and the abbey and perhaps we can visit for a weekend together."

"Maybe next Spring? I hear they have really beautiful gardens too."

"Sounds like a plan."

They were about to join the motorway and Cooke turned on the radio to listen to some music, which had a calming effect, and traffic bulletins which would warn him of any possible holdups. Alice, who found motorways boring, took out her current read and settled back to enjoy it.

The journey was uneventful and three hours after leaving home they arrived in the centre of Bath, where Cooke pulled over to the side of the road.

"I'll give you a bell when I'm ready to pick you up. Have a good time."

"I certainly will! I hope your enquiries are productive. See you later."

It didn't take long to reach the village of Little Bathington, and after negotiating the narrow lane which constituted the main street Cooke found the turning he was looking for and drew up behind a grey Toyota. His knock at the sky-blue wooden door was soon answered by a man of average height, dark haired with just a touch of grey at the temples. He was wearing designer jeans and a polo shirt with the unmistakable logo of a high-end brand.

"Mr Lawrence? DCI Cooke, Derbyshire police." He showed his warrant card.

"Come on in. I was just about to have coffee, if you'd like to join me. We could talk in the garden."

The smell of freshly ground coffee hit Cooke as he followed through the kitchen and out into the courtyard garden beyond where he took a seat at the wrought iron bistro table. While he waited, he gazed about and noted two wooden planters filled with pansies, and a couple of sparrows politely taking turns to help themselves to seeds from a feeder hanging from an ornamental cherry tree.

"How do you take your coffee?" Lawrence called through the open window.

"Black, no sugar please."

Lawrence sighed as he sat down, having placed two mugs on the table.

"Firstly, I'd like to say how sorry I am for your loss," Cooke said.

"Thank you. I can't believe she's never coming back."

"How long had you been married?"

"Eight years last month."

"Can you think of anyone who might have wished to harm Valerie?"

"No, no-one. She was a really quiet, home-loving woman and just wouldn't upset anyone."

Tears filled his eyes and Cooke waited a moment for him to compose himself. "When did you last see your wife?"

"A week ago last Friday, at breakfast. She phoned me at work later that morning to tell me she needed to go up to Derbyshire to her mother's. The old girl had an operation recently and needed help at home for a few days. She left while I was at work."

It seemed she'd lied about why she was going to be away, and Cooke wondered why.

"Can I have her mother's address, please?"

"It will be in the address book. I'll go and get it, but I rang her yesterday to let her know. She was pretty shocked, as you can imagine." He left the room, returning a few minutes later.

He flicked through the pages before handing the book to Cooke.

"She phoned me back to tell me she would be staying with her sister for a few days and gave me her mobile number so that I could let her know when the funeral would be. I feel really guilty now because I didn't ask her on either occasion how she was."

"Under the circumstances I doubt she will have noticed you didn't ask."

"This is going to sound really awful, but I really didn't want to talk to her at all. I blamed her because if Val hadn't gone all the way up there to look after her she'd still be alive."

"Did you speak to Valerie during the week she was staying with her mother?"

"Yes, she rang me every evening to keep me updated."

"When was the last time you spoke to her?"

"Friday. She told she was coming home Saturday."

"Did you try to ring her on Saturday evening when she hadn't turned up?"

"I tried her mobile but I got a message from the provider saying it had not been possible to connect my call."

"Did you try her mother's landline?"

"No. I didn't want to worry her."

"Did Valerie work?"

"She left her job in the city a couple of months ago. I've got a well enough paid job and she really didn't need to work."

"Where did she work?"

"Boothby Anderson in Bath – she was in marketing."

"Did that take her away from home at all?"

"Her job was office based, in charge of the department, so there were others who did the leg work. She did go to Yorkshire in May; the firm were opening up a new branch so she was up there scouting for local products."

"Do you have the dates she was away in May?"

Lawrence consulted the calendar on his mobile phone.

"She was away for two weeks from the seventh of May."

Cooke made a note. He would check if the dates corresponded with the Italy trip.

"Did she phone you while she was away that time?"

"Yes, every day. Luckily she had a works mobile with her because she left hers at home. She told me she couldn't find it when she was about to leave so I set it up so we would be able to find its location in future."

"Did you meet any of her colleagues?"

"She didn't mix with her colleagues outside of work hours, preferred to get home at the end of the day, so no, I never met any of them."

Cooke took a sheet of paper from his inside pocket and opened it out on the table and asked, "Do these dates mean anything to you?"

"No, what relevance are they?"

"They were blocked in on your wife's phone. Does she have a diary here?"

"I'll go and look in her bureau."

He soon returned empty-handed. "I can't see one but I couldn't open the little drawer where she keeps her passport. It may be in there."

Cooke remembered the small key on her key ring.

"I believe you fell out on Friday evening over her taking on a house-sitting task starting Sunday?"

"She'd been away all week, and I was missing her."

"Were you aware that your wife had taken future house-sitting assignments?"

"Yes and no. I knew she was thinking of doing a spot of house-sitting and had agreed to a couple. I wasn't keen on her being away but in the end I agreed. I work from home but often have to go to site meetings which can be anywhere in the country. I might have been able to join her and make a bit of a holiday of it."

"Can I ask you where you were on Friday evening?"

"I was here at home all evening."

"Alone?"

"Just me and the cat."

Cooke rose to his feet. "I'll keep in touch, and we'll courier your wife's belongings to you in due course. In the meantime if you think of anything which might help us with our enquiries give me a call." He reached into his inside pocket and produced a card.

Back in his car Cooke looked up Boothby Anderson on his phone and found they were a company collating and distributing local products from the West Country in the form of hampers. He rang the number, introduced himself and asked to speak to the manager.

Sharon made an early start by ringing Tour2Explore Holidays and a very helpful clerk quickly located the passenger list for the tour in question and emailed a copy through. There were forty-four passengers in total, mainly married couples and friends who had booked together, plus six single bookings. Having spoken to Amanda she now wanted to speak to the other singles she had spent mealtimes with, hoping that while chatting they might have gained some valuable insight into Valerie's character.

She looked through the list three times before she narrowed down the six people who had dined together. The only one she managed to find at home was Mary Ridley, the retired school mistress. Sharon introduced herself and gave a brief outline of why she was calling and how she was trying to get a better picture of Valerie Lawrence.

"We were an unlikely bunch of companions," Mary chuckled.

"In what way?"

"We were all so different and had very little in common, but saying that, we all got on well together and certainly had a good laugh every night."

"What can you tell me about Valerie?"

"She had been seated by Amanda on the coach and they were like chalk and cheese, but they chatted happily and stayed together during the daytime when we visited all the wonderful sights that Italy had to offer. Seemed the perfect holiday companions, but after Valerie's little mouse had gone to bed that cat sure knew how to play. She was the life and soul of the party, and she did like to flirt with the men in our little group."

"Can you tell me more about them?"

"There was Adrian, an art student, and definitely gay. They sat me next to him, and boy, was he hard work! I have to say I'm glad my days spent as a teacher were with juniors. He didn't speak much and was always reading about the next place we were visiting in his Lonely Planet; followed our journey on a big map, which was a blooming nuisance half the time. Whenever I saw him out and about he was taking photographs."

"She flirted with him?"

"Yes. I really don't think she realised that he wasn't interested in women."

"Who were the others?"

"Giles and Steve. They were much more *interested,* shall we say. Giles had been made redundant from a warehouse job and had used some of the money for the holiday; he was hoping to hear from a national company who were recruiting for their new store. Steve was recovering from an acrimonious divorce and told us he usually enjoyed golfing holidays with his mates. He'd won this holiday in a raffle, and although the prize was for two had nobody who was available to join him."

"Thank you for your help, Miss Ridley."

"You're most welcome. I've enjoyed having someone to talk to and it's allowed me to reminisce."

Cooke was glad that Alice had printed off a map of the city centre for him and he soon found a car park close to where he'd dropped her off. It was a short walk up Southgate Street and past the Roman Baths to the address he was looking for. At first it wasn't obvious how to get to the first floor where the offices were situated above a row of shops, but on closer inspection he found a door between a boutique and a café with the logo he was looking for. Steep, narrow steps led him to an office with a small reception desk immediately in front of him. Although open plan, the space was sectioned by clever use of furniture. Magnolia walls and tall windows added plenty of light.

Warrant card already in his hand, he walked up to the desk where a young girl was seated at a forty-five-degree angle and facing a computer screen. She looked up at his approach and smiled.

"How can I help you?"

"DCI Cooke. I'm here to speak to Mr Taylor."

"Ah yes, he's expecting you. Take a seat over there and I'll ring through to him."

She pointed at some comfortable-looking grey fabric-covered chairs grouped in a semi-circle around a round low table where fliers on the company were left for perusal. Cooke picked one up and flicked through it absentmindedly. He didn't have to wait long before a smartly dressed man appeared by his side, hand outstretched to greet him.

"I'm Steven Taylor, General Manager. We spoke earlier." Turning to the desk, "Claire, can you bring some tea through please?" he said. "This way, Chief Inspector."

Cooke was led into a large area at the far end of the office completely surrounded by glass partitions, rendering it a separate unit while appearing to be part of the whole.

"Take a seat. You wished to ask about Val? We were devastated to hear of her death."

"Had she worked here long?"

"She'd been with us fourteen years and was a real asset to the company."

"Did you notice any difference in her after she married?"

"Not really. She was the same hard-working young lady, who got on well with everyone. For a couple of months beforehand she'd stopped joining her colleagues on a Friday night after work and I'd heard she'd got a new boyfriend, but we were all rather taken aback when she came back from a week's holiday and announced she was married."

Claire arrived holding a tray with two cups of tea, an individual milk pot and sugar sachet in each saucer along with a spoon.

Cooke poured milk into his drink and took a sip before asking, "She seemed happy?"

"Yes, I'd have said so. It was a shock when she handed in her notice. She said that she'd been offered a job elsewhere."

More lies, Cooke thought.

"You obviously weren't expecting her resignation?"

"No. It was clear she loved her job and I was surprised she wanted to leave. At the time I wondered if maybe her husband was behind it."

"Are you planning to expand the business in the near future?"

"Maybe we'll bring some more products on board. There are some wonderful producers in this part of the world."

"But nothing like another branch?"

"No, it doesn't do to get too big. Too easy to take your finger off the pulse."

Cooke finished his tea and wished that a biscuit had been forthcoming.

"Thank you. I wonder if I could speak with some of the people she worked with now."

"Yes, of course. I'll take you back to the waiting area. That's as good as anywhere for you to talk to them."

Cooke was struck by how quiet an office of this size could be, everyone working diligently, and even the phones having a soothing soft ring – so different from what it was like in the main office at the police station. But then, the police didn't have the same sort of budget for office space as a private company.

The first person to approach was a dark-haired woman who looked to be in her late thirties and introduced herself as Anne. She only echoed what he'd already heard; Valerie was a hard-working, happy woman whom everyone liked. A few more of her colleagues had little more insight to add, until a man called Mike came and sat down. He was slightly older than the others, and it soon became obvious that he didn't seem to have as high an opinion of Valerie as the rest.

"I wondered if she was as happy at home as she made out. She hardly knew him after all when she up and married him and dumped poor old Terry."

"Terry?"

"Terry Smith. They were so good together and we all thought they would marry one day, but when she met Charles Lawrence she dropped Terry like a stone. He was heartbroken; he was as sure as everyone else that it would be him that she would meet at the altar. He used to join us in the wine bar on a Friday night and became one of the gang. She stopped coming after she took up with the new man, and so did Terry."

"Do you know how I can get hold of this Terry?"

"He owns Hearty & Fresh, the gourmet bistro in the next street, really good wholesome grub using local ingredients. Some of the girls went there for afternoon tea and said his pastries and cakes were to die for."

All this talk of food made Cooke's stomach rumble and he decided it would be a good idea to meet up with Alice for lunch, and an ideal opportunity to speak to the ex-boyfriend, so he asked Mike for directions.

Once outside the building, he phoned Alice and arranged to meet her at the bistro, which was situated on the corner of two streets and with plenty of windows offered a bright well-lit interior. Although it was a weekday the place was busy, but they were soon able to secure a table. The waitress handed them the à la carte menu along with a card detailing the specials which offered two or three courses at a fixed price. They both chose items from the latter.

"It's a nice little place," Alice commented as

she looked around properly at the minimalistic but classy decor. "How come you chose this venue? Has it got good reviews?"

"It was recommended by someone I was interviewing this morning, but there is an ulterior motive as I want to speak to the owner. His name came up in conversation and I think it could be worthwhile."

"I might have known," Alice rolled her eyes.

When the girl brought their drinks Cooke asked if Terry was available.

"He's busy in the kitchen at the moment," she said, looking at her watch, "but things slacken off around two. Who shall I say is asking?"

"DCI Ben Cooke." He showed her his warrant in a way that wouldn't be seen by other diners. Seeing her face change he added, "I only want to speak to him about someone he once knew."

"I'll let him know."

"So how was your morning?" he asked his wife while he took a gulp of his bottled beer.

"The Jane Austen Centre was even better than I thought it would be. All the staff were dressed as characters and the introductory talk was very interesting and entertaining. The guides all had humorous tales of Jane and her family as we wandered through the different rooms. She was a real trail-blazer in her time, in an age when authors were predominately male. The costumes were wonderful and everyone is encouraged to dress up." Alice grabbed her phone and soon found a photo of herself in a beautiful blue Empire-line dress, posing with someone she said was Mr Darcy.

"Very nice," Cooke said, glad that he hadn't had to dress in the man's outfit.

The starters arrived and after setting down Alice's pancake, stuffed with mushrooms, bacon and Somerset brie cheese, the waitress told Cooke, "I'll take you through when you've finished your meal."

"Thank you," Cooke replied, picking up a piece of sourdough bread toast to spread with the homemade paté and red onion chutney.

The couple chatted happily as they ate their meal, and Alice left in search of Bath buns while Cooke paid the tab and waited to be summoned to a little office next to the kitchen.

"I'm sorry, my waitress didn't tell me your name, just that you are a detective."

"DCI Cooke from Riversmeet Constabulary in Derbyshire. I'm looking into the death of Valerie Lawrence and was hoping, as you were once close, you may be able to help me get a better picture of her as a person."

"It sounds strange to hear her called that; she'll always be Valerie Shaw to me."

"How long were you together?"

"Five years. I was planning to ask her to marry me once I'd got this place up and running and making a profit."

"Did you accompany her when she went to stay with her parents?"

"At Christmas and Easter and special occasions like her mum's birthday, but otherwise I was too busy."

"Did she act any differently when she was with her family and friends back home?"

"No, she was the same old Val, always smiling and happy."

"When did you last see her?"

"To speak to, on the night she broke up with me. We'd been out to the cinema and I thought she was unusually quiet. It was a weeknight so I didn't expect her to stay, but I wasn't prepared to hear her tell me it was over. I had no idea there was anything wrong so it hit me for six. Turned out she had been out with that creep a couple of times."

"You said 'to speak to'. Have you seen her since that night?"

"Nearly every day at first because she always passed here on her way to work. She didn't see me watching her through the small kitchen window. I knew what time she would pass by and it was a habit which stopped when she married him because she never came this way again. Up until then I clung onto the hope that she'd see the error of her ways and come back to me."

"Will you go to the funeral?"

"I thought about it, but it would mean closing this place for the day, and for what? It wouldn't bring her back."

There was a knock and a lad in kitchen gear looked around the door.

"Sorry, Terry, but there's a couple who want a late lunch. Can we take them?"

"I'll be out in a minute." Terry looked at Cooke for confirmation.

"Just one more question. Could you tell me where you were on the evening of Friday 7th October?"

"Here, finishing up and planning the specials menu for the next day. I usually get home around eleven thirty."

"Would there be anyone with you?"

"No, the staff go home when we close."

"Thank you for your time." He got up to leave and added, "My wife and I enjoyed our meal very much. "

"Thank you, good to hear. Leave a review on Trip Advisor," he grinned as Cooke left and he hurried back to the kitchen.

CHAPTER 11
Friday 14th October

There was a light mist swirling as Cooke drove into town and a definite autumnal feel in the air as he walked from his parked car towards the police station.

Seeing him enter the room, Jimmy held up a print-out. "The information has come through this morning from her phone provider. I've only just started looking at it, but it confirms that she phoned her husband every evening. The last call to his number was last Friday."

Cooke looked at the obvious fingerprints on the printout and guessed that Jimmy was still catering for himself courtesy of Greasy Joes café. What he needed was a good woman, but then again where would they find a woman who would put up with him?

"Keep at it, lad. Wendy, run a search for a Terry Smith on the system, owns a bistro called Hearty and Fresh in Bath."

"On it, sir."

He was eager to talk through his thoughts

on Lawrence with Sharon and found her on the phone, busily taking notes. She waved and he nodded by way of greeting as he walked to his desk and sighed at the sight of the teetering pile of paperwork waiting for him. Once seated he reached for the topmost item and had managed to go through the overtime reports, agreed Golding's two weeks' leave for next May and glanced at the new target directives before filing them in the bin, by the time Sharon finished her call.

"What did you think of our Mr Lawrence?" she asked.

"He seemed to be holding it together pretty well most of the time, but I could tell he was struggling. On the surface, at any rate, he seems genuine enough, and although it wasn't a complete waste of the trip I don't think I'm any closer to getting to know his wife. I'm not even sure how well he knew her – he thought she was in Derbyshire visiting her mother, which poses the question of why she hadn't told him the truth."

"Perhaps she thought he wouldn't like her house-sitting so far from home."

"Possibly. I went to speak to her previous employers and the manager told me she advised them that she'd been offered another job when she handed in her notice; they were shocked as she'd seemed so happy there and he thought the husband may have had something to do with her decision."

"Curious."

Cooke nodded. "Everyone liked her and spoke highly of her, all except for one man who told me about how she had dumped her previous boyfriend of some standing when she met the man who was to become her husband. I think it was a friend of his, which may have swayed his judgement. It seems that she stopped socialising with her work colleagues once Lawrence came on the scene so there might be something in what the husband told me about her not having any friends."

"Any more," Sharon finished the sentence. "The boyfriend could be a person of interest."

"I actually went to speak to him, and he seemed a nice chap. Runs a pleasant little restaurant in the city and says he's moved on, but I got the impression he still held a torch for her. I've got Wendy looking into him. He says he would have been working alone on the next day's menu after they closed then went home. We'll see what CCTV shows up but even if he left at closing time he would have been hard pressed to get up here in the timescale."

"Since I spoke to you on Wednesday I've been trying to get hold of the other singles who had become pals on that holiday, to find out what they had to say about our Valerie, and it seems unlikely to me that she didn't have friends. As I told you, Amanda was surprised to hear that Valerie was married because she had told them she was a widow. The only one I spoke to yesterday was an older, retired lady who described her as the life and soul of the party once Amanda had gone to her room, and a proper flirt with the three men even though one of them was obviously gay."

"Either her husband really thought she didn't have any friends, or he didn't want us talking to them."

"Or maybe he's a control freak." She rifled through her notes. "I've just spoken to Steve, another of the holiday singletons, who according to my retired lady is a keen golfer. I asked him if he had ever been to the Wellsend Golf Club and he told me he hadn't, said he played locally to him in Essex and went to Spain or Portugal with his mates once or twice a year. He confirmed that Valerie was a bit of a flirt and said he got the impression that Giles had probably scored with her. He also said she arrived at dinner late one night and seemed a bit upset and subdued."

"You've not spoken to Giles yet?"

"No, I left a message on his mobile but he hasn't returned my call. I'll try again."

"It will be interesting to know what this Giles has to say. I have to report to the chief so I might as well get it over and done with."

With no good news for his superior Cooke left as Sharon picked up the receiver and began to dial.

"I don't know how they expect a better conviction rate on burglaries when we don't have enough manpower," Cooke muttered as he threw a report he was carrying into the waste paper bin to join the others. "Any luck?"

Sharon shrugged. "Not really. I've left another message."

"Well, let's hope he responds to that one. Coffee? I'm buying."

Sharon nodded, grinning.

He returned from Brian's Den with two Danish pastries as well as the drinks.

"Thank you. Now I'll need an extra hour at the gym tonight." Sharon took a bite before continuing, " I've just had a very interesting conversation."

"I'm all ears."

"Adrian, the young student, did not like Valerie Lawrence. He said he'd caught her out on quite a few lies during the holiday. Silly little things like one afternoon they booked in early at the hotel and he heard her tell Amanda that she was going for a lie down, then he saw her sneaking out as soon as her friend had gone to her room. He wasn't at all surprised to hear that she wasn't the widow she claimed to be, said she wore a cheap but pretty ring on her wedding finger most of the time, which didn't quite cover the pale mark another slightly bigger one had left; but later she wore a gold infinity ring on that finger. He'd admired it and she said it was just costume jewellery she'd picked up at the market in Sorrento the day before, but it so obviously wasn't. "

"Sounds like the ring she was wearing when she was found, and that certainly wasn't from a market. A very complicated woman to fathom out. We know more about her but know nothing about her. Different people see a different woman as if she changed to suit the person she was with – something of a chameleon. When we can find out who the real Valerie Lawrence was we might get a better idea of a motive which led to her death."

CHAPTER 12

Saturday 15th October

The alarm went off at six o'clock, and after a quick breakfast Cooke took Buster the short distance to K9 Kennels for what was described as a VIP stay. This weekend had been planned a while ago; Alice was looking forward to meeting up with her family in the capital to celebrate her sister's fiftieth birthday. Although he enjoyed going to the theatre, Cooke wasn't so keen on musicals - too much singing and not enough action, but there was also afternoon tea to look forward to and a full English breakfast tomorrow at their hotel. With little in the way of strong leads at the moment, his team were quite capable of getting on with things in his absence, and it would be good to escape work for the weekend.

Letting the train take the strain, Cooke was pleased to see the skies brightening as they made their way south, and just over two hours later they stepped out of St Pancras station into bright sunshine.

After booking into their hotel, Cooke told Alice

he had a surprise for her, and she was delighted when, a short tube trip later, he revealed that he had secured fast-track tickets for the London Eye.

Sharon didn't like missing anything which might be relevant to the case and was interested enough to want to follow up on the gold infinity ring, to find out if it was actually from Italy and how much it was worth; so she signed it out and set off to an independent jeweller in town. She went to school with him and knew he'd built up a reputation locally as a fount of knowledge on antique and modern gold jewellery.

The door bell chimed as she entered the shop, which was empty except for Nathan, who looked up and smiled in recognition.

"Well, if it isn't Sharon Whittaker. What brings you to my humble workplace?"

Sharon showed him the ring and asked him what he could tell her about it. He looked carefully at it through his magnifying loupe.

"It's definitely Italian, gold but only 14K, a simple infinity design. It would still cost up to two hundred pounds in this country."

As he handed the ring back he took a quick glance at her left hand.

"No rings on your fingers I see. Still single then?"

"Married to my job, mate. Work and a family life just don't mix. The divorce rate for coppers is high.

After enjoying a light lunch near Leicester Square, Cooke and Alice walked via Trafalgar Square to Covent Garden where they had plenty of time to wander around the arts and crowd with his magic skills, before meeting up with her family for afternoon tea nearby.

Cooke wasn't impressed by the crustless dainty sandwiches and would have preferred a pint to the champagne, but he enjoyed the cakes and scones on offer. Alice was glad he was blissfully unaware of the cost.

A couple of drinks later in Shaftesbury Avenue, Cooke was chatting to his brother-in-law, Roger, as they walked to the theatre.

"I remember watching *South Pacific* with my parents years ago. I thought it silly the way characters suddenly broke out into song," Cooke told him.

"I know what you mean, but it's different at the theatre, the music is part of the story. *Les Miserables* has a great storyline , and the score is wonderful. You'll love it, old chap."

"The jury is still out on that one. I'll let you know later."

As they arrived at the theatre Roger asked where Cooke and Alice were staying.

Cooke told him and added that it was handy for the station.

"We're staying just around the corner from you, so we might as well share a cab after the show."

Cooke had been intending to go by tube but readily agreed. It had never occurred to him to take a taxi, but it struck him that other people did it all the time. Something tickled at his memory; he'd assumed that Valerie had been picked up by someone she knew, but she could have gone by taxi and met that person elsewhere.

CHAPTER 13

Monday 17th October

"How was your weekend?" Sharon asked Cooke as she breezed into the morning meeting.

"Very good. I think I could actually get to like musicals."

After hearing his grumbling last week, Sharon gave him a look which said she wasn't convinced.

Cooke clapped his hands and looked around at his assembled crew, waiting for them to pay attention before speaking.

"We are no nearer finding the identity of Valerie Lawrence's killer but we have a slightly better idea of what sort of person she was. It seems that she was a lady who was rather economical with the truth. When I spoke to her husband, he told me she had come to Derbyshire to look after her mother after a stay in hospital, which was clearly untrue. He said she had no friends, but she was a sociable girl by nature so I find this hard to believe. By all accounts she loved her job but a short while ago she handed in her notice, telling her employers she had been offered alternative employment – another lie. We know she went on a coach holiday to Italy in May, telling her husband she had to go to Yorkshire, to help set up a new branch of the firm she worked for."

"A way of meeting one of her friends?" Wendy suggested.

"She obviously didn't want him to know about it, although as far as we can ascertain she didn't know anyone on the tour so may just have needed some time away. Sharon has been speaking to some of the other passengers on the coach and for some reason she portrayed herself as a widow who had been left comfortably off by her late husband. Quiet at first, she was soon mixing well with the others and enjoying their company."

"Sounds like she was enjoying her freedom," offered Golding.

"Anything on Terry Smith, Wendy?" Cooke asked.

"Nothing to report. He seems squeaky clean."

"He seemed a nice chap but it was obvious that he still loved her and he doesn't have a solid alibi. Had any useful sightings, Tom?"

"Wendy and I have been following them all up, but there have been a lot of time wasters. We've got a few to do this afternoon after my radio interview. Another customer thought she had spoken to her in Chapter and Verse, the independent bookstore, earlier in the week so we'll go there, and finish up at the Bunch of Grapes Bistro where she might have been on Friday night."

"Mention the car, Tom, say we'd be interested in hearing about a silver car which may have been seen parked up near the golf course in the days leading to the murder. Sharon, I want you to concentrate on contacting all the local taxi firms, find out if any of them picked Mrs Lawrence up on the Friday evening. Jimmy, anything more on her phone?"

"Yes, in view of what you have just told us, it might be relevant. I noticed that every call she made home was at precisely 6pm which I thought was maybe a bit odd; but I found evidence to suggest that the phone location was possibly being tracked."

"Charles Lawrence told me she was apt to losing her phone and he'd set it up so that it could be found easily. Presumably she would have been aware of this," Cooke replied. "Wendy, can you arrange for the rest of Valerie's belongings to be picked up from the Watsons and go through it all as you bag it up, just in case there's anything of interest that we've missed."

On that note Cooke and Sharon left the room. As they neared the bottom of the stairs they met Truman coming from the front desk area, about to head up to their office.

"There's a man out there says his name is Giles Hammond, wanting to speak to DI Whittaker."

"Thanks, Truman. Show him through to the green room."

In fact the whole interior was painted in a

rather unattractive green, but the one Sharon alluded to was the friendly interview room. She went to join him once she had collected her notepad and pen.

"Good morning, Mr Hammond," she said as she entered. "Thank you for taking the time to come and see me."

"I could have phoned, I suppose, but as I don't live far away and I hadn't got anything planned I thought I'd come in person."

"As I said in my message, I just wanted to ask a few questions about the coach holiday you went on in May."

"Fire away." Hammond stretched out his legs and assumed a relaxed manner.

"I believe that there were six single people who sat together at dinner every night."

"That's right. All the other folk were couples so we were all ushered toward the last table together."

"Was it awkward or did you all get on well?"

"It worked surprisingly well. Mary was the gang leader or mother hen. She very soon had us laughing at her tales of life as a school teacher and the 'little darlings' as she called them. Some of the things primary school children get up to and say," he shook his head, smiling. "I told her she should write a book."

"Did any of you spend time together outside of mealtimes?"

"I was sitting by Steve on the coach but we went our own separate ways once we were dropped off. Adrian was a bit of a geek, didn't speak much but when he did he bored the pants off everyone, so he went off on his own with his camera. Mary was off the coach like a whippet with her itinerary already mapped out for every stop. Amanda and Valerie sat together and wandered round together off the coach, although they didn't know each other beforehand."

"What were Amanda and Valerie like?"

"Totally different. Amanda was quiet and went up to her room after dinner, while Valerie was a live-wire and joined the rest of us in the bar."

"Would you say Valerie was a flirt?"

"A bit. She certainly lost her inhibitions after a couple of drinks," Hammond grinned.

"Did she come on to you?"

"No more than with the other two. Why?"

"It's been suggested that you may have had a brief affair."

Hammond sat up and a frown was quickly replaced by a smile.

"Well, it would have been nice but it never happened."

"I'm told you all spent the evening together after dinner on the last night."

"Yes. We were at Lake Garda and had a very early start the next morning. We all, including Amanda, went to a bar by the lake for a farewell nightcap."

"Did you exchange addresses, phone numbers?"

"Lord, no. We were on holiday. It was over, end of."

"So you haven't seen or spoken to any of the others since that holiday?"

"No."

He ran the back of his hand across his mouth.

Sharon looked at her note pad.

"I think that's all. Thank you for your time, Mr Hammond."

"Can you tell me what all this is about?"

"I'm sorry to have to tell you that Valerie was found dead last Saturday and we're speaking to people who knew her to try and get a better picture of the sort of person she was. Nothing for you to worry about, sir."

"That's awful. It sounds like you think she was killed?"

"It looks that way, sir."

Sharon got up and showed him out, then went straight through to speak to Jimmy.

"Jimmy, do a search on Giles Hammond for me, see if he's got a record. I'm sure I've seen him before somewhere."

"Well? Any more light shed on our mysterious woman?" Cooke greeted her when she returned to the office.

"Not really, but there's something familiar about Mr Hammond. Jimmy's doing a check on him."

"I had a phone call when you were speaking to him." He handed her a piece of paper with a few lines written on it. "Red Vauxhall Corsa, local registration, although the person who rang this through couldn't say whether it was 55 or 65, and she wasn't hundred percent sure whether the second letter was a D or an O as she was standing too far away, not wanting to be seen by the driver. She had noticed it at the end of Robin's Close on more than one occasion when she was going to clean at a house nearby and thought it strange because there was someone sitting in it each time. They didn't get out – just sat there. She couldn't see the driver although she was certain it was a man as on one occasion a hairy arm was leaning through the open window."

"Sounds interesting. I'll get Wendy to do a vehicle search."

It didn't take Wendy long to find a vehicle which fitted the bill.

"It belongs to one Victor Cash and is registered to an address in Wellsend," she told him, passing him the details.

"Very interesting. I think I'll go and pay Mr Cash a visit."

Cooke passed the red Vauxhall as he made his way to the front door of the terraced house. It would have been called a council house back in the day but would now be referred to as social housing. What passed for the lawn of the long front garden was strewn with kids' bikes and other outdoor toys, and he could hear a woman chastising someone as he rang the bell.

The door was answered by a clearly harassed woman, dressed in leggings and long baggy tee shirt, her dark greasy hair dragged back into a ponytail. She looked less than pleased to see a stranger on her doorstep.

Cooke introduced himself and showed his warrant. "Mrs Cash?"

"That's me," she answered, hands on hips.

"I'm looking to speak to Mr Victor Cash."

"He's not back from work yet. What d'you want to speak to him for?"

Cooke ignored the question.

"How long will he be?"

"What's the time?" She looked at her watch. "Any minute. He's a creature of habit and he's never late for his tea. You'd better come in, I s'pose."

He was shown into a living room where a huge television was showing some cartoon and two young lads barely registered his presence as they carried on playing electronic games, the noise of which was very quickly grating on Cooke's nerves. He was relieved to hear the woman yell to their father as the front door slammed.

"There's a detective in the front room wants to speak to you."

Cooke stepped out into the hall to meet him. "Is there anywhere quieter we could talk?"

"Come on through to the kitchen. We can sit at the table."

Mrs Cash sighed as they walked in. "Your

tea's nearly ready. I may as well go and get the washing in while you talk." She huffed, snatched a washing basket from the worktop and stomped out, slamming the door behind her.

"What do you want to talk to me about?" Cash asked as he sat down heavily at the table, meaty arms crossed.

"You are the registered owner of the red Corsa on the drive?"

"So? It's all taxed and insured."

"It has been seen several times on the Birds estate in Ashthorp and has been reported to us as suspicious."

"I'm a carpenter. I have done quite a few jobs round there recently."

"I would have thought you would have needed a van for your tools and materials."

"The van blew its head gasket and was in the garage for well over a week before they got it back on the road. Bloody nuisance having to use the car. Missus wasn't too pleased as it meant she had to walk the boys to school."

"There's a good golf club here, isn't there? Do you play golf at all?"

"Nah, that's not for the likes of me. I like football – watching it, that is."

Cooke couldn't quite imagine the man in front of him actually playing football.

"Have you ever been to the golf club?"

"No way, you've gotta be joking. All snobs and arse lickers."

Cooke showed him a photo of Valerie Lawrence.

"Do you recognise this woman?"

Cash looked at the photo and shook his head.

"I couldn't tell you who she is, but she does look familiar. Does she live in Ashthorp? Was it her that reported my car?"

"No, she was murdered."

"Murdered! Hang on a minute. I saw something about that in the paper. That's where I've seen her before – in the Herald." A worried look came over Cash's face. "Is that why you're here asking me these questions? I didn't know her, I've never met her. I've done nothing wrong."

"In which case you've got nothing to worry about."

Mrs Cash bustled through with the basket, now stacked with laundry, on her hip, looking pointedly at Cooke.

"Well, I think that's all, Mr Cash. Thank you for your time."

Cooke got up and saw himself out. He'd ask Sgt Greaves to send his boys to check out Victor Cash's account of having been working in the area.

CHAPTER 14

Tuesday 18th October

Sharon popped into the office early to leave a note on Cooke's desk to tell him she'd be back in time for the meeting. The golden morning sunshine filtered through the changing leaves in the local park and Sharon thought that it made them look even more beautiful.

She arrived at Clive's Cabs and introduced herself to the harsh-faced blonde behind the screen.

"I've come to speak to Phillip Moore." She showed her ID.

"He won't be long. I had to send him on a short job up to the bus station."

There was little room in the office so Sharon wandered outside to wait. A large silver saloon came round the corner and parked alongside her. A young lad leapt out and dashed past her into the office, but was soon back out again, and approached her with a smile.

"I'm told you are looking for me – Pip Moore."

"Is there anywhere we can go to talk?"

"We've got a driver's lounge, but believe me, you don't want to go in there. Better to get in the cab." He strode round to the passenger door and opened it for her.

Sharon took her note pad from her bag and made a start. "You were on duty on Friday, 7th October, and were given a job to pick up a Mrs Lawrence from Skylark Drive and take her to the Italian wine bar in the main square?"

"Yes, I remember that one because when I picked her up she asked me if I could take her to the railway station in Riversmeet instead. I rang in the change and took her there."

"Did she tell you where she was going to?"

"I didn't ask. She paid and walked off, and I thought there might be a possibility of a new fare if a train was due, so I pulled onto the taxi rank for a while. When I looked out I saw her again but she wasn't going into the station. She was walking further into the car park. I might be wrong, but it looked like she was meeting a man that was standing by a red hatchback."

"Could it have been a Corsa?"

"Could have been."

"Can you describe the man?"

"It was dark so I couldn't see his features. Casually dressed in what looked like jeans and a sweatshirt. A bit taller than her, around five ten I'd say."

"Any idea of age?"

"No, sorry."

The radio crackled into life with a voice asking if anyone was available to do a pick up from Tesco's.

"Have you finished?" Moore asked.

"I think so, but if you think of anything else that might be useful please get in touch." She handed him her card and could hear him accepting the job as she got out of the car. Before he had chance to drive off Sharon made a note of his number which ended in 60TAP. She would check it against the file but thought this could very well be the car seen by the Watsons' neighbour.

Cooke found Sharon's note, and turned his attention to a couple of reports. Reading the first he found that Golding had spoken to the barmaid at the Bunch of Grapes who had seen a woman answering Valerie's description early on the Friday night; she had arrived alone but went to join a gentleman already seated in the dimly lit booth in the corner. He'd obtained CCTV footage and would look at that this morning.

The other was from Wendy who, armed with a copy of the photo, had spoken to the manager at Chapter and Verse. He'd taken it and said he would make sure all the staff saw it, and would let her know if it jogged anyone's memory. He wasn't very hopeful as they'd been very busy with a book signing on Wednesday which had generated a lot of work but not a lot of interest. There were no security cameras in the shop.

The phone starting ringing and gave him a reprieve from starting on his in-tray. It was the lady who had been expecting Valerie to house-sit for her last week returning his call having found the message he'd left on her answer machine. She had managed to persuade her daughter at the last minute to make a diversion on her way to work each day to feed the cats and had only returned from Menorca late on Sunday. She was a bit concerned as when her daughter arrived at the house on the Wednesday morning she had found a man lurking in the garden. He seemed to think that Valerie Lawrence lived there. Cooke took down the daughter's details and would ring her this evening to get a description of the man.

While he was waiting for Sharon, Cooke finally made a start on his paperwork. A recent spate of burglaries in local villages had all been well-planned and executed and despite house-to-house enquiries, no-one had yet been apprehended. The local councillor had cried foul and had been bending the commissioner's ear, which in turn meant that Cooke was going to be on the receiving end of a loud and somewhat harsh complaint. He could do without that, and it sent his mood even more downhill.

He threw his pen onto the desk and stomped down to speak to Golding. As he walked into the room he found Wendy in the process of sorting through Valerie Lawrence's possessions.

"Found anything of interest?"

"Nothing special, just the sort of things anyone would take for a few days away."

"Once you've been through it, get it packed up and couriered to her husband."

Golding and Jimmy were watching the CCTV footage from the Bunch of Grapes and glancing at the screen he found they were still scrolling through the lunch-time images.

"Any feedback from the press interview?"

"A few more possible sightings, which I'll follow up this morning, but I think we can rule out the speeding car. A lady rang to say her husband had been rushing her to hospital on the Friday night and had possibly been going a bit too fast on that piece of road, causing another car to take evasive action. They got there just in time for the birth of their first child, who I could hear exercising its lungs in the background."

"It was always a bit of a long shot," he shrugged before heading for the door to return to his den.

"Sir!"

He turned round to see Wendy with a light jacket in her left hand and waving something in her other.

"What have you found?"

"A small Nokia, in her jacket pocket."

"Have a look at this, Jimmy. It might prove more useful than her main phone."

Glad to find Sharon had returned, he was keen to update her about the finding of the Nokia.

"It will be interesting to see what Jimmy can winkle out of it," she said.

"Also, the house-sit lady phoned me back and, to cut a long story short, it seems that a mystery man visited what he thought was Valerie's home while she was supposed to be there. I'm hoping to speak to someone tonight who can give me a description of him."

"Interesting."

"Anything useful from the taxi driver?"

"She'd booked to go to the Italian bistro in town, but when he picked her up she changed the destination to the railway station."

"Any idea where she was going?"

"She wasn't actually catching a train. He hung about the car park thinking that if there was a train due he might get lucky and pick up a fare and saw her heading towards a man stood next to a red hatchback - could be Corsa man. What did he have to say for himself?"

"Turns out he's a carpenter and has been working in Ashthorp recently. His van was off the road so he was using the family car while it was at the garage. Still, what you've just told me still puts him firmly back in the frame."

He looked at his desk and the mound of paperwork and groaned. He was restless and needed to be doing something more constructive so picked up his keys.

"I'm going to see if Councillor Booth is at home. He's the latest victim of our prolific burglar and he's making a lot of noise about the incompetence of the police."

Councillor Booth was not in the slightest bit pleased to find him on his doorstep. "Come in, but I haven't got a lot of time as I have a site meeting with the playground developers at eleven."

He hurried through to his office, a room off the spacious hall. Cooke could smell fresh paint as he followed him and found the room was full of boxes on the floor and several surfaces.

"Excuse the mess. We've been having some work done. I must say I'm surprised that someone of your rank would come and pick up the list, particularly as the constable asked us to bring it to the police station."

"We're taking this spate of burglaries very seriously, and I actually came to ask you some questions, but I'll take the list if it's ready."

Cooke took the printed sheet and scanning through it saw there were several pieces of silver as well as jewellery, which was a diversion from the thief's normal cache of money and easily grabbed tech items.

"Do you have photos of the jewellery and these silver candlesticks?"

"Yes, we had some taken for insurance purposes. These things are of great sentimental value for my wife and I."

He went to a drawer in the filing cabinet and retrieved an envelope. "I have another copy of these, so I don't need them back in a hurry."

Cooke would take them round to Fingers Findlay, their friendly neighbourhood pawnbroker.

"I've read the report on your burglary. You found that your house had been broken into while you were away for a few days. I have to ask you if there was anyone, besides friends, that knew you would be away."

"I may have told the painter when we were fixing a date for him to start on the living room."

"And could you give me his details?"

"Yes, his card is on the fridge door, I'll go and fetch it."

He was soon back and handed Cooke the card.

"Had you noticed any strangers in the neighbourhood recently such as door-to-door salesmen, leaflet drops, or a car you didn't recognise?"

Booth shook his head.

"You cancelled any regular deliveries - newspaper, milk?"

"We don't have milk delivered, and we had asked Harry next door to push through any newspapers or post, but sadly he suffered a heart attack and was taken into hospital while we were away. We were surprised to see all manner of paperwork sticking out of the letterbox when we came back."

"It's the sort of thing these villains are looking for."

"Actually, I've just remembered something.

The missus had a text to say that something she had ordered had been delivered, and that was still on the doorstep when we got home. The burglar broke in through the French windows at the back of the house so he can't have noticed it, or he would probably have taken it too." Booth glanced at his watch. "I really do have to leave, so if that's all?"

"If there's anything else you think of that could be of help, please give me a call." Cooke reached into his inside pocket and produced his card, and was hastily ushered to the door.

With all their hopes at the moment pinned on finding something useful on that new phone or on the CCTV footage, sitting around waiting was not an option. Cooke called Sharon and asked her to rally the troops for a meeting for when he returned and all except Jimmy were waiting in the main office when he arrived.

"Where's Jimmy?" Cooke asked Sharon.

"He'll be here shortly. We can start without him."

"We are getting nowhere fast in this investigation and every path we have uncovered has led to a dead end. Firstly, has anyone got any good news for me?" He looked around.

"I've found a very good frontal shot of Valerie's companion as he was leaving and Jimmy is going to tart it up and make it clearer," offered Golding.

"Good work! Get it out there as soon as possible."

"I'll have it on social media by this evening - surely someone will recognise him."

"Let's hope so."

"I've been looking at footage from the railway station and although there is no clear shot of the man Valerie Lawrence was talking to, I can confirm that the car was a Corsa," Wendy informed them.

"Good work."

At this moment Jimmy arrived. "Sorry I'm late, I met our boys in blue on my way here. They have been speaking to local residents around the Birds estate in Ashthorp to check out Cash's story, and it seems that he had indeed recently completed several small jobs for different households on the estate."

Cooke sighed as that backed up that suspect's alibi for being there, but he still wasn't ready to rule him out.

CHAPTER 15
Thursday 20th October

With Alice away at her mother's for the night, Cooke had enjoyed a solitary brandy before hitting the sack to help him get off to sleep. He'd woken early with a start and very soon realised that it had been thunder that had disturbed him when the room was lit up with a flash of lightning heralding another resonating crash. He counted one, two, three, four, five before the next rumble - the storm was moving off to the east but the diminishing tempest was now replaced by rain beating on the UPVC window sill. The bedside clock's red digital figures indicated 5.30. Knowing that there was no likelihood that he would be able to go back to sleep, he decided to get up.

Golding had released an enhanced copy of the full-faced clip from the CCTV footage on social media last night and Cooke was eager to find out what, if any, response it had received, so his first point of call was to the civilian who had been manning the desk and incident line overnight. Although there had been a few calls from people who had been in the Grapes that Friday, nobody had come up with a name yet. Feeling hungry and disappointed, he needed something to cheer him up, and having missed out on breakfast he found himself heading for the canteen with a full English in mind.

Replete and in a slightly better humour, he headed upstairs to his workstation and found Sharon waiting impatiently for him. She hardly gave him chance to get inside the door before imparting her news.

"I've just spoken to our friend Oliver Watson," she greeted him. "He knows who Valerie met in the Bunch of Grapes."

"So who was it?"

"Only the same person who had recommended that she housesit for him. His work colleague, Christopher Shaw."

"Interesting, and definitely a person of interest. Is he at work today?"

"Yes, they both work at the sports shop on the West Trading Estate."

Cooke already had his car keys in his hand.

"No time like the present."

The rush hour traffic was against them, and it was a frustrating journey across town with Cooke's patience being well and truly tested; but finally they pulled up near the store.

"Can I speak to the manager please?" Cooke asked a female assistant who was arranging football shirts on a rack near the door. The girl looked at him for an instant and sensing this was an official request rather than a customer complaint went off and returned with a smartly clad fellow, who, clocking them, looked worried.

"How can I help you?" he asked.

"DCI Cooke and DI Whittaker," he showed his warrant. "We'd like to speak to one of your employees – Christopher Shaw."

"Chris is out the back taking a delivery."

"Is there anywhere we could speak to him alone?"

"You can use my office, but I'll warn you it's a bit cramped."

"Lead the way."

They followed him through to a room at the back of the shop.

"Chris is one of our older employees. Steady bloke – I can't imagine why you would want to speak to him."

Cooke didn't enlighten him.

He showed them into a sparsely furnished cubbyhole where a phone sat on a small desk next to a pile of catalogues carrying logos which Cooke recognised as some of the big names in sportswear.

"Take a seat. I'll go and fetch him."

"It is rather bijou," Sharon commented as she looked around.

There were only two chairs so Sharon took the seat behind the desk and Cooke leaned on the small windowsill, leaving the other chair facing them for Shaw. After a short wait a figure appeared in the doorway. Cooke was pleased to see that this certainly looked like the man on the CCTV footage.

"The boss told me you wanted to talk to me."

Cooke introduced himself and Sharon and bade him sit down.

"We have some questions for you, as someone has identified you as a person that Valerie Lawrence met at the Bunch of Grapes on Friday October 7th."

"Yes, we met for a drink and a catch up before she went back home."

"We think you may have been one of the last people to see her alive."

"You can't think that I would harm her, surely."

"We aren't accusing you of anything," Sharon told him. "Can you tell me how you knew Valerie?"

"Val is – was my sister; well, half-sister. She asked if she could come and stay with me for a few days but I only live in a small flat and don't have enough room, so when Oliver mentioned wanting to take his missus away I suggested her house-sitting for him."

"Did she give a reason for the visit?"

"She wanted some time and space to think."

"Why here?"

"She told me that she was seriously thinking of moving back up this way to be nearer to her mum. She hadn't told her anything about her plans because she didn't want to get her hopes up."

"Do you think she was planning to move up

here alone or with Charles?"

"She didn't say but I assumed she meant both of them. She'd been looking at the job market in the area. He mainly works from home so could work from anywhere in the country."

"How did you get on with Charles?"

"I only ever met him the once at Dad's funeral and didn't really have much of a chance to actually talk to him. Val stayed by his side the whole time and hardly spoke to anyone, which was strange as she's usually such a gregarious person."

"How did she seem when you met up with her at the Bunch of Grapes?"

"Much more herself. Really chatty and said she'd bumped into an old friend earlier in the week."

"Did she say who?"

"No, and I didn't ask. Perhaps I should have?"

"No reason why you should. She didn't say whether she'd made any arrangements to see the person again? "

"No, she was in a bit of a hurry to get off and I assumed she'd got to pack and possibly tidy the house before leaving the next morning."

"Did you both leave the pub at the same time?"

"Pretty much. I stayed a bit longer to finish my pint and went home."

"Thank you, Mr Shaw. We may want to speak to you again. If you give us your home address and phone number we won't have to bother you again at work."

Cooke noticed what neat handwriting the man had as he wrote down his details on a page torn from the notepad on the desk.

Handing it over Shaw said, "I feel so responsible. If I hadn't suggested the house-sit, she might not have been here. She would still be alive."

"Don't blame yourself," Sharon told him.

CHAPTER 16

Friday 21st October

Rain was pelting down as Cooke negotiated the narrow country lanes to the village where Mrs Shaw, Valerie Lawrence's mother, lived. The heater was failing to clear the mist clinging to the windscreen and it was too chilly today to put on the air-con.

He negotiated a small stone bridge over a little brook and the houses of the village of Bees Cross came into view, neatly clustered around one side of the village green, which the road split in two. Sharon pointed out a couple of white goats which were tethered on the other side as Cooke drew up and looked around for inspiration. As with a lot of villages, the houses had names rather than numbers and they were looking for Pear Tree Cottage. Under the expanse of Cooke's large umbrella they started up the track which serviced the dwellings and after passing several charmingly named cottages, Sharon noticed one with a tree espaliered to the frontage, so they made their way towards it and were rewarded with a sign on the little wooden gate declaring it to be the one they were seeking.

The path leading to the front door of the cottage had a neat garden either side where Michaelmas daisies, various chrysanthemums and bright pink cosmos vied for attention with dahlias and a clump of nerines.

Cooke folded his umbrella as Sharon stepped into the porch and rapped the green woodpecker doorknocker. She heard a chain slide into place before the door was opened a crack and a woman's voice asked who her caller was. Sharon confirmed she was speaking to Mrs Shaw and introduced them both, holding up her warrant to the gap.

The door was opened fully to reveal a woman who Sharon guessed to be in her early seventies with short grey hair and dressed in black trousers and a clearly hand-knitted jumper.

"We'd like to ask you some questions about your daughter, Valerie," Sharon told her.

"You'd better come in then." Mrs Shaw stepped to one side. "Could you put your brolly in that pot please." She indicated a vintage brown glazed earthenware jar. Cooke complied and they were led into a low-ceilinged room with very little light from a small wooden framed window, where they were invited to sit down.

Choosing the floral covered sofa facing the hearth, they sat side-by-side at right angles to the chair deemed to be the one Mrs Shaw preferred as her knitting lay next to it on a highly-polished round table. She sat down heavily, her whole demeanour one of sad resignation.

Cooke opened the conversation. "Firstly, I'd like to offer our condolences on your loss."

Mrs Shaw looked beyond him, blinking away the threatened tears. "Thank you," she answered quietly.

"We know that Valerie didn't stay with you while she was up in Derbyshire, but did you see her at all?"

"Oh yes, she came to see me every day for afternoon tea. I love baking and she never could resist my homemade cakes."

"When was the last time you saw her?"

"On the Friday afternoon. I'd made her favourite, chocolate brownies, and I gave her some to take home the next day. I've been baking this morning, but there's too much for me. Would you like a slice of cake? I'll go and put the kettle on."

She was out of her seat and heading for the door before he had time to reply. He'd have preferred to get on with the interview but had long realised that it created a more relaxed atmosphere if refreshments were involved.

While she was gone he looked around the room and admired the black painted beams and the old stone fireplace, which was laid ready to be lit. He thought this room would be really cosy on a cold winter's night. Sharon stayed seated, while he wandered over to look at the few paperbacks on a shelf next to the padded window seat, half a dozen Catherine Cookson and a couple of Mills and Boon, before inspecting a landscape print of a rural scene on the wall. An old black and white wedding photograph in a silver frame took pride of place on the sideboard – Mrs Shaw and her husband, he assumed.

"That looks like Valerie," he commented as he pointed to a young girl in a gown and mortar board.

"There isn't a photo of her and Charles' wedding though," Sharon remarked.

"Nor the brother," Cooke replied.

The tea and fruit cake arrived, and once it was duly shared out Sharon asked, "What time did Valerie leave on Friday?"

"About half past six. She always rang Charles before she left each day on the mobile she kept here during her stay."

"Wouldn't she need it?"

"Oh no, she had an old work mobile she could use when she was out and about. She was always worried that she might lose hers as it had all her banking details on it, so she left it here to keep it safe."

"Did she say where she was going?"

"She said she needed to go back to the house and feed the rabbits and then she was meeting a friend."

"She didn't say who?"

"No, dear, she didn't. I assumed it was an old school friend."

"She met up with her brother for a drink when she left you. She didn't mention she was meeting him?"

"Chris? He's her half-brother. I'm rather surprised that she would be seeing him. They were never that close."

"Did you see Valerie often since she moved south?" Cooke took over again.

"We did at first, but once she got married she wasn't able to come so often. She was working all week and obviously wanted to spend time with Charles at the weekends. They were busy doing up the house in their spare time. They came up together for Bert's funeral, but she usually came on her own when she did get time."

"Do you have any relatives in Chipping Norton?"

Mrs Shaw looked puzzled. "No, we haven't many relations left and what there are still live around here."

"Do you know why she was house-sitting on this occasion?"

"She told me she was doing it as a favour for a friend."

"Her husband thought she was staying with you."

"Silly man, must have misheard her. She probably told him she'd be able to come and visit me."

"Do you think he might not have liked her house-sitting up here without him?"

"By all accounts he's happy in his career and often has to go away on business so why would he mind?"

"Did you meet her former boyfriend, Terry Smith?"

"Yes, he often came up to visit with her. Lovely lad and doing well for himself, I believe. Bert and I were shocked when she told us that it was over between them. We really liked him."

"How did you feel about her marrying Charles?"

"I liked Terry and had hoped they might have got back together. Bert and I went down for the wedding. I was surprised when I found out we were the only family invited. My sister was really hurt. They'd always been so close."

Mrs Shaw stared into space, obviously lost in some memory.

"Well, I think that's all," Cooke said. "We'll be on our way. Thank you for the tea. The cake was delicious."

Sharon agreed and they both got up to leave and were escorted to the door.

The rain had stopped and Cooke almost forgot to pick up his umbrella on the way out.

"Well, what did you make of that?" Cooke asked as he started the engine.

"I'm sure Mrs Shaw was being honest with us, but whether Valerie was being so with her is debatable. I still think she was planning to leave Charles and was doing the groundwork to be self-sufficient when she did so."

"I'm inclined to agree with you. I think she had a mutually agreed time to ring her husband so visited her mother at the same time every day because she knew her location could be tracked when she used her mobile."

Cooke popped into the main office for an update on their return to base, while Sharon went off to type up her notes.

Jimmy had opened the Nokia but all texts and phone history had been deleted. He would have to wait for details from the service provider.

CHAPTER 17

Friday 23rd October

After a night of excruciating toothache Cooke had managed to secure himself an appointment with Alice's private dentist later this morning. He wasn't a regular visitor to such an establishment, having been traumatised by the school dentist years before, and wouldn't be going now if the pain killers had worked. Consequently he was not in the best of moods as he counted down the hours in his office.

After a light knock Alf, the front desk clerk, popped his head round Cooke's door.

"Yes?" he snapped, in no mood for visitors, and immediately felt guilty at being so abrupt. "To what I do I owe this pleasure? I don't usually see you up here."

"Sir, I've had a phone call from a Mr Johnson, who lives in a little hamlet called Bee's Bridge, and has just returned home from a couple of weeks holiday. He was talking to his neighbour this morning who warned him about all the recent burglaries, and he remembered a car he'd seen hanging around one afternoon the week before he left, although he couldn't remember which day it was. It didn't belong to any of the neighbours and he'd thought it strange enough at the time to write down the number plate." Alf handed Cooke a piece of paper. "He didn't know what make it was but said it was light grey."

"Where was this?"

"Bee's Bridge."

"Thanks, Alf. Could be the lead we need to finally catch our prolific house-breaker."

Cooke accompanied the desk clerk downstairs and made his way straight to see Wendy.

"Can you find out who owns this vehicle?"

"No probs."

Cooke wandered over to the window which looked out over the car park at the back of the building. It had started to rain and already puddles were forming in the uneven surface. He could see Sharon dashing from her car, with her handbag held ineffectively over her head.

"It's registered to Minerva Construction of Bath, so will be a company car."

"Bath! That's a bit of a coincidence, and I don't believe in coincidences. "

Cooke checked the large-scale wall map of the local area. He found Bee's Bridge, and spotted the village of Bee's Cross about a mile downstream. A footpath followed the brook from the hamlet into the village.

"If that car was Lawrence's company vehicle,

he would have been able to leave it there and walk to where he believed his wife was staying."

Back in their office Cooke updated Sharon as she combed her bedraggled hair.

"At first I thought it was a lead on our thief, but being so near to Bee's Cross... Lawrence is a commercial architect so it's possible he could be employed by Minerva Construction."

"If it was him, there can only be one reason he'd be in the vicinity of his mother-in-law's home and that would be to check up on his wife. Perhaps he didn't like what he saw," she reasoned.

"And if it was him we certainly need to speak to him again. Give them a ring and find out if he works for them, and if so whether that is his company car. I have a date with the dentist."

"I thought you didn't believe in dentists."

"I don't." He pressed his hand to his aching jaw, and scowled.

Sharon grinned as she picked up her mobile to look up the number for Minerva Construction and pressed the call button.

The brave soldier arrived back from the torture chamber face numb and minus one molar, and still smarting from the lecture he had been given about taking more care of his teeth.

"How did you get on with Minerva?" he mumbled.

Sharon hid a smile. "Lawrence is in charge of

drawing up the plans for the shopping complexes which they build, but he's employed by them on a freelance basis so doesn't have a company car. The vehicle in question is used by Bill Davis, their go-between with the relevant council. They have a contract to build a small row of shops with flats above in Skepmead so he had good reason to be in these parts, although that's some fifteen miles from where his car was spotted."

"There's still a link, Lawrence may have asked him to pop round to give his wife a message or he might have arranged to meet Valerie himself. We need to speak to him and find out what he has to say for himself."

"That's what I thought, so I've asked them to get in touch with him and tell him to contact us."

CHAPTER 18

Monday 25th October

Opening his drawer to look for some staples, Cooke found the envelope given to him by Councillor Booth days ago. He'd forgotten about it, and decided he'd better go and see if anyone had offered them to the local pawnbroker Shane Findlay.

He found him polishing an ornate lady's pocket watch which he was planning to put in his window display.

"Hello Shane, how's business?"

"Not too bad. What can I do for you, Mr Cooke?"

Cooke opened the envelope he was carrying, took out the photographs and fanned them out on the counter.

"Been offered any of these?"

Shane Findlay wiped his hands on the back of his jeans and reached for his spectacles before picking up each picture to study it.

"Some good stuff here, but nah, I haven't seen anything of it. I'll keep an eye out, but I'd be surprised if I do. Most of those sort of 'heirlooms' tend to end up on line these days."

"Well, let me know if anyone shows them to you."

"Will do. Can't interest you in a lovely fob watch for the missus?"

"She's got a smart watch."

"It's not an everyday watch, it's a piece of art."

"I'll still pass."

It was late morning when Cooke returned to his office, and he was pleased to see his lunch, ordered earlier from Lettuce Eat, the favoured deli of his team, waiting for him. His jaw still ached from where the gum deadening needle had been administered the day before and he found it difficult to open his mouth fully to accommodate his longed-for beef and horseradish sandwich. The phone started ringing just as he'd managed the difficult manoeuvre.

With Sharon in court this morning, he had to answer the call himself. He was glad he'd only managed a small bite.

"DCI Cooke."

The caller had a broad accent which he took to be Bristolian. "Hello, this is Bill Davis from Minerva Construction. I'm told you'd like to speak to me."

"Ah yes, thank you for calling. I'm dealing with a serious incident in my area of Derbyshire, and we've been told that you've recently been working on a new project at Skepmead."

"Yes, it's all signed and sealed now, and work begins next month. There's not a problem, is there?"

"No, it's nothing to do with the development. Your car was seen in Bees Bridge during the week ending Saturday October 8th. Could you tell me why you were there?"

"Certainly. I'd finished at Skepmead and thought I would look up a distant cousin. My wife had been working on her family tree for the grandchildren and had started looking at mine. I don't have many family left, so when she found that a branch of the family had moved that way years ago, I was keen to speak to a living relative."

"What's your cousin's name?"

"Mark Swain."

"Can you give me his address?"

Cooke wrote it down.

"Did you go to Bee's Cross while you were there?"

"As a matter of fact I did. It was a nice sunny day, and my cousin suggested we take a walk around where his parents had settled and where he'd lived as a child, so we took the footpath along the river to that village."

"Did you visit anyone while you were there?"

"No, his father died some years ago and his mother is in a care home. He showed me the cottage where he grew up and we went to the church and had a look round."

"Were you aware that Charles Lawrence, the company's architect's mother-in-law lives in the same village?"

"Well, I never! No idea at all. What a small world it is."

"Do you know his wife?"

"Never met her. I liaise with Charles on projects and attend the same meetings, but we don't socialise outside of work."

"So you weren't aware that his wife was up this way that week?"

"No, why would I be?"

"He might have mentioned it."

"We are both busy men. We only talk work."

"I think that's all for now. Thank you again for calling."

"I still don't understand why you're speaking to me?"

"We're investigating the death of Mrs Valerie Lawrence."

"Dead? Hell's bells – so that's why the last meeting was postponed. They didn't say."

Cooke thanked him for his time and ended the call.

Although he was inclined to believe Davis, Cooke would still check out the existence of Mark Swain.

CHAPTER 19

Wednesday 26th October

A brainstorming session was well under way in the main office when Janet, the civilian manning the incident phone this morning, walked in and stood waiting to speak.

Cooke finished his sentence before turning to her. "Yes?"

"Sorry to interrupt, but I've got someone who says she was a friend of Valerie Lawrence on the line. She'd like to speak to someone on the case."

"I'll take it," said Sharon, following her out.

Cooke turned back to the assembled team.

"So it would appear that Lawrence works freelance for Minerva Construction and as such does not use a company car. The driver of the vehicle seen in Bee's Bridge professes not to know Valerie or that she was in the district. I've checked his account of why he was there, and he was indeed visiting his long lost cousin."

"We know Valerie last phoned her husband on the Friday evening, a phone call which ended on a sour note. Could he have driven up to make amends?" Golding asked.

"It's a three hour journey on a good day but we only have his word that he took the phone call at home so it is possible," Cooke replied.

Sharon returned, and Cooke looked up expectantly. "Anything useful?"

"It could be. Kay Sharpe was a friend of Valerie's from before she went to study at Bath University, where she met Terry Smith and ultimately moved south to be with him. She was calling from work but said she'd be able to pop in later."

"Could be she has more information about young Terry too," Cooke replied.

"Thank you for coming to speak to us, Ms Sharpe. This is DCI Cooke, who is leading the investigation." Sharon indicated for her to take a seat.

"I need to catch the six o'clock bus so I can't stay too long."

"You said you had some information for us."

"As I said on the phone, I don't know if I can be of much help, but I can't help thinking about the night when Val was killed."

"You said you were a friend of Valerie's," said Sharon.

"Yes, I've known her like forever."

"And you've kept in touch since she moved away?"

"Yes, we'd usually meet up when she was

visiting her mum, and sometimes I would go down and stay with her, before she met Charles. I mean, it wouldn't be the same staying with a married couple, would it?"

"But you stayed with her when she was with Terry?" Cooke asked.

"Yes, I liked him and was never made to feel in the way."

"So you didn't feel the same about Charles Lawrence?"

"I've never met him. I wasn't even invited to the wedding, which upset me at the time, but Val later told me that it had been a very low-key affair at a registry office with only very close family. I was surprised really because she'd always wanted a big wedding and we'd planned on being each other's bridesmaid."

"So you met up while she was up here at the beginning of October?" Cooke prompted.

"I went for coffee with her on Thursday morning to discuss my staying with her at one of her house-sitting jobs."

"When were you planning to stay with her?"

"She'd got a house-sit in Birmingham at the beginning of December and I was going to stay with her the 8th and 9th. We were intending to visit the big Christmas market there."

"So what can you tell me about the Friday night after you met your friend for coffee?"

"We'd arranged to meet up with the rest of the gang at Giardino del Vino on Friday evening, but she phoned at the last minute to say she'd be a bit late and to start without her."

"Did she say why?"

"Not exactly. I'll get to that in a moment, but I need to go back to our conversation in the café on the day before."

"Fire away."

"She told me she'd had a brief fling a while back. She and Charles had been going through a bad patch and she'd gone off the rails a bit. She said that it didn't last long and that she and he were now as happy as they ever were. The thing is, she'd been shocked to see the other man when she was shopping in Riversmeet on Wednesday."

"You say the affair didn't last long. Did she tell you who ended it?"

"Yes – she did. She'd seen sense when he'd started getting a bit clingy, and buying her gifts. She hadn't wanted anything serious."

"Did she mention his name?"

"I asked her but she said I wouldn't know him. Anyway, she literally came face to face with him and there was no way she could avoid speaking to him. He asked her out to dinner that night and really seemed keen to rekindle their romance but she gave him some excuse about having to be elsewhere. When she phoned me on Friday evening she told me she'd be a bit late as there was something she had to sort out – no, 'put straight' was how she put it."

"And you think it might have had something to

do with the man she met on the Wednesday."

"I don't know, but she sounded agitated, and it has crossed my mind several times since."

"She didn't tell you anything about him, like was he someone she knew from her hometown?"

"No, but he could have been; she was certainly surprised to see him in Riversmeet, that's for sure. There was someone who she used to work with who was rather sweet on her. Now what was his name?" she frowned, then shook her head. " Sorry, I can't remember."

"She had a stepbrother - do you know him?"

"He was some years older than us, at senior school already when we started primary school, so I never really knew him as such. I rarely saw him, but I do remember him being really nasty to Val's mother when I was round her house one day. I don't think he and Val got on very well then, but like most of us with older siblings I think they actually became friends later on, once she'd moved away."

Kay glanced at her watch.

Cooke noticed and wound up the interview.

"Thank you again for coming in. You've been very helpful."

"I'll see you out," Sharon offered.

"Well, what do you think?" she asked as they walked back into their office.

"I've just checked and there is a week blocked off on Valerie's calendar from 3rd to 10th December and the dates which Kay has just given us for her visit match the asterisks."

"Looks like she was using her house-sitting as a way of meeting up with her friends."

"Which makes you ask why she felt the need to meet them away from home."

"Most likely because she didn't want her husband to know," Sharon reasoned.

"He did tell me she had no friends and I think he believed it was true."

"I wonder if anyone else knew about the affair, and whether it was someone from work or elsewhere."

"It could be relevant, but unless we can find out who he is it hardly helps make anything any clearer," Cooke replied.

"Maybe we can forget about the husband now."

"Not entirely; he might have come up on the Friday evening to check on her and saw them together. We only have his word about where he was that Friday evening with nobody to confirm it. She always rang him on his mobile so he could have taken the phone call anywhere. At least we know she was in Riversmeet shopping on Wednesday so we need to get all the CCTV footage we can from that day. We might get lucky and find that meeting. The shops she went into need to be followed up, and any security camera footage too."

"What about Chris Shaw? I think we should look a bit further into their relationship. He had helped her by finding the house-sitting job, and they met up that night."

"I think it would be useful to speak to the mother again. She was surprised to hear that her daughter had met up with him."

CHAPTER 20

Thursday 27th October

It was a cold clear morning and the sun was beaming down from a cloudless blue sky. Cooke had phoned ahead and was enjoying his drive to Bee's Cross. A red kite swooped low across the road in front of him, thwarted from securing a meal as his car approached. The village itself took on a friendlier face today and the brook shimmered in the valley as it flowed towards the little stone bridge. He was soon at the village green, and strolled up the steep track to the cottages beyond.

Mrs Shaw was next to the garden gate cutting back the stalks of a Michaelmas daisy plant which was now past its best, and spotting him, she put her secateurs on the wall and waited for his arrival before leading him round to the back of the house, and in through a small conservatory to the kitchen.

"It was so good to see the sun this morning, I felt I needed to take advantage of it and get a bit of tidying up done," she told him. "Take a seat."

Without asking she turned the kettle on and

spooned loose tea from a tin into a brown teapot, while Cooke took a seat at the small round kitchen table on one of two Sixties-style wooden chairs.

"I'd like to ask you about your stepson," Cooke said as she poured boiling water into the pot.

"Chris? I don't really see much of him," she answered, taking a large plastic box from a shelf above the work surface.

She placed a china plate with a large slice of Victoria sponge and a small fork in front of Cooke and leant on the back of the vacant chair before carrying on, "He was always a difficult child. I really tried with him, but we never really bonded. He was six when I married his dad. His parents were already divorced when I met Bert, and he lived with his mother at first, but then decided he wanted to come to us. She had a new man in her life and was quite happy with the arrangement. At first things were okay, that is until Val came along. He resented her, and me more so. He had a cruel streak, and I was forever having to step in and play referee. "

"We've spoken to him, and they seem to have been on a more friendly footing recently."

"Really? She didn't say, but then why would she? She would probably have felt she was betraying me in some way. Although he did seem to see her in a different light when she reached puberty, if you know what I mean, and I was glad when he moved out."

"I can see how that would have been a worry

for you. Was there anything specific?"

"The way he looked at her, in particular. Then she started to become secretive and would tell such fibs. Apparently she'd told the whole class that her dad was a brain surgeon and that we lived in a huge house in the country. I found that out when I went to the school to a parent/teacher evening. I confronted her the next day, but she flatly denied it."

"So things haven't got any better between you and him with the years?"

"I'm afraid not. He always bore a grudge about being upstaged by Val. She was such a daddy's girl, you see, had him wrapped around her little finger. I haven't had any contact with him since his father passed away. Of course, he still used to visit while Bert was alive, but it was as if I wasn't there half of the time." She turned away to pour the tea.

Cooke took a forkful of cake and waited until she had placed the mugs on the table and sat down heavily opposite him, sighing as she did so.

"When she told you she was house-sitting for a friend, that wasn't completely true. It was Chris who suggested she do it for a colleague of his. You seemed surprised that she had met him after she left you on the Friday."

"I was. She told me she was meeting a friend but it must have been him."

"In view of what you have told me about their relationship, do you think he could have wished her harm?"

"You don't think–?"

"We can't rule anything out."

She considered it, but then shook her head. "No, I don't think he would. I can't say that I like him, or ever will, but Bert is dead and buried now so he can't see either of us as a rival for his father's attention. I'll probably see him at the funeral next week. I will be civil and I hope he can be too."

"Did your husband leave him anything in his will?"

"No, everything was left to me. I really ought to get a will made up, but it's one of those things you tend to put off, isn't it?"

"Thank you for speaking to me again. That cake was delicious."

"Would you like another slice to take with you? It's no trouble."

"No, thank you – I'm supposed to be cutting back," he told her, his recent visit to the dentist preying on his conscience. He got to his feet and took his leave.

The journey back to Riversmeet had been made difficult by the low sun shining brightly into his eyes, and at times he had to slow right down to a crawl. He arrived back at the station with his head thumping and made his way straight to his desk, searching in vain through his drawers for some painkillers.

Sharon wandered in with a cup of vending machine coffee.

"Would you like one?" she asked.

"No thanks, I've been well catered for by Mrs Shaw."

"Cake too, I wouldn't wonder."

"Victoria sponge actually, and very nice it was too. Have you got any paracetamol?"

Sharon picked up her bag and handed him the remainder of one strip of pills which he swallowed without the aid of water.

"So what did Mrs Shaw have to say about her stepson?"

"There's no love lost there. He seems to have seen her as the evil stepmother and didn't get on too well with her daughter when they were younger. She seemed to think that, with his father now gone, it is unlikely that he would harm his half-sister, but I'm not so sure. We know he was with her that evening and they parted when she left the pub, but we don't know that he didn't follow her; he's got nobody to back up his alibi that he spent the rest of the evening at home alone. It's not beyond the realms of possibility that it was him she had a brief fling with."

"You know what they say about absence making the heart grow fonder."

"I also asked her mother whether he'd been provided for in his father's will and apparently everything was left to her. She hasn't made a will yet and with Valerie out of the way a step-son would be able to make a claim on Mrs Shaw's estate."

"Maybe we should have another chat with him."

"Let's hold fire on that for now. In the meantime, ask Wendy to look at any cameras that could have picked up her journey after she left the Grapes. We know she went home but we need to try to find out if she was followed."

CHAPTER 21

Wednesday 2nd November

It was Quiz Night at the Cat & Fiddle in the village of Frogwell, and the Bullfinches team had arrived late, meaning the only table left was the one right next to the door which led to the toilets. Although they had done well tonight and were sharing the luxury chocolates which constituted second prize, Julie Bull noticed her friend wasn't quite herself this evening.

"You seem miles away tonight, Sally. Is there anything wrong?" she asked.

"Sorry, no, nothing like that. I've just got something on my mind."

"Can we help at all?"

"Thanks for the offer but it's nothing, just something the boss has asked me to do."

She wanted to tell Julie; they'd been friends since primary school and she knew she could trust her, but Gina, who was also on their team, was well known as being as big a gossip as her mother. She couldn't risk this getting out as she didn't want everyone to know it was her that had named someone from their own village in relation to the murder that had been all over the local paper. Her chance came when Gina went to the toilet.

"You remember that woman that was found dead at Wellsend?"

"Yes."

"My boss asked if anyone had seen her in the shop last week, and I'm sure it was her that was talking to – let's just say, someone from this village, and she seemed pretty friendly with him. I've been given the morning off to go and speak to the police."

"Who was it?"

"I really don't think I should say. It was probably innocent and I don't want to get him into trouble. I can't imagine him hurting anyone and I don't want to go to the police station."

"You have to go," Julie touched her arm. "It's the right thing to do."

"Where you got to go to?" Gina asked as she sat down.

"Er – Jury Service." It was the first thing that came into her head. Her uncle had been called up last month.

"Well, you do have to go then."

It was after ten when the three girls left for home. A fog had descended and the streetlights were surrounded by halos as they walked beneath them, chattering and giggling as they passed the few shops and closed curtained houses of the village high street until they reached the church gate which marked the parting of the ways. Julie and Gina lived on the council estate in one direction and Sally a couple of hundred yards up Church Street.

Cooke looked at his watch, and was surprised to see it said ten past twelve. Where had Thursday morning gone?

"Wasn't someone from that bookshop supposed to be coming this morning?"

"The manager rang yesterday to confirm that a Sally Green would be in to see us, yes. He said he'd given her the morning off to do so as she was reluctant to tell him who she'd seen Valerie speaking to," Sharon replied.

"We'll give her a bit longer; morning could well mean anything up to one or two o'clock to some people."

"I would have thought most people would want to come early and get it over and done with."

"Give her until two, and if she doesn't show perhaps you should go and pay her a visit at work."

Cooke turned back to the pile of reports that never seemed to go down. At last one of them actually came up with something interesting.

"Our burglar has struck again, but this time he's left the scene empty-handed and injured. Seems he must have cut himself on the patio door; there was a skid mark on the stone slabs nearby and it looks like me laddo smashed straight into the door. Forensics have gone to take samples and from the amount of blood at the scene he could have needed stitches. Owners were out last night and didn't go into the living room so only found the damage this morning."

"I'll give the A&E department a little visit. With waiting times as they are, you never know – with any luck he might still be there," Sharon said.

"No, I'll go. I could do with some fresh air and I'd rather it was you who spoke to the shop assistant. She'll be more at ease with you than me."

Cooke arrived at Accident and Emergency and scanned the people in the waiting room as he waited for the receptionist to finish speaking to a harassed mother whose young son had fallen from a swing and had probably broken his arm.

He introduced himself and asked if there had been anyone treated since the night before with a nasty glass wound. She looked at the log and found that indeed someone had.

"He told the nurse he'd slipped and fallen into the greenhouse. He was stitched up and sent on his way."

"Do you have his details please?"

"Name of Trevor Wingrove, of 52 Broad Street, Riversmeet."

"Thank you."

Cooke would pay him a visit.

Again Cooke was blinded by the low sun and flipped the visor down, to little effect. Every year he promised himself he'd get some sunglasses, but he never did. He found a space in Broad Street outside a newsagent's just big enough to squeeze his motor into without touching the yellow lines, made a note of the number 12 on the wall by the door and started walking past a couple more shops before he came to the first of the houses which was number 18. He passed number 34 and came to the cemetery, but after that the road sign told him he was now entering Cherry Tree Lane. Another wild goose chase! The villain had given a false address, and name too, he suspected.

Before driving back to the station he nipped into the newsagents and came out brandishing a family size bar of chocolate. He broke off a large chunk which went some way to appease his frustration.

His office was empty when he got there and he found a note from Sharon telling him that Sally Green had not turned up to see them and that she was going to the bookshop to speak to her there.

I'll bet she just took the morning off and never thought we'd follow up on it, he muttered to himself.

It was already dark when Sharon returned, and Cooke had just turned off his computer ready to head home.

"You've been a while," he greeted her.

"It wasn't as straightforward as I'd thought."

"Tell me about it. Our man had been to the hospital but gave a false name and address to the medics."

Sharon groaned.

"I went to Chapter and Verse and asked to speak to Sally. They said she hadn't turned up for the afternoon shift."

"A bit cheeky taking the whole day off."

"There's more. I spoke to the manager and with some difficulty was able to persuade him to give me her home address. I drove straight round and spoke to her mother who told me Sally wasn't there. When I asked her when she'd seen her last, she told me that Sally had gone to the Pub Quiz last night with her mates and when she wasn't home this morning, thought she'd probably stayed at her friend Julie's house, as she quite often did. She rang Julie's mum while I was there to check and was told that she hadn't been there. Now the woman's in a dreadful state. I brought her with me, and she's downstairs filing a missing person report."

CHAPTER 22

Saturday 5th November

Wrapped up in warm coat, bobble hat and matching scarf, the little girl was holding on tightly to her dad's hand as they entered the field behind the community centre. In front of them her dad could make out the large mound of the bonfire silhouetted against the night sky. Close behind them his wife followed, carrying the packet of sparklers.

Soon after their arrival the countdown began for the village dignitary to set light to the accumulation of old pallets, cardboard boxes and various other items which made up the centre-point of the evening's festivities.

"Five, four, three, two, one!" the crowd chanted, and very soon flames were licking around the pile, illuminating the crowning glory wedged up against the topmost pallet.

"Look, someone has put a Guy on top." The man pointed to the very top of the bonfire.

His young daughter knew all about Guy Fawkes and how he had tried to blow up the

Houses of Parliament because her teacher had told them all about it at school yesterday.

"It wasn't there earlier when I took Max out for his walk," his wife commented.

Everyone was enjoying the warm glow while they waited for the firework display.

There was a scream as the Guy slid down the burning slope of the fire onto the ground yards away from spectators who were luckily standing well back behind the safety rope.

The crowd was soon distracted as the first of many rockets shot up into the air and a shower of red stars burst and crackled into life above. While Catherine wheels were spinning, Roman candles displaying their pretty colours and rockets whooshing high in the air, children enjoyed making patterns with their sparklers.

As the last huge chrysanthemum rocket faded to leave just stars twinkling in the clear sky, the villagers left the glowing embers and made their way to the community centre where homemade soup and hot dogs were waiting.

The younger children and their parents drifted off home, leaving only a few stragglers enjoying the last of the mulled wine while the caterers for the evening were clearing up. Old Joe, the community centre's caretaker, wandered out to make sure the bonfire was safe to leave.

He had taken down the ropes and was about to start raking the ashes when he found the heap of burnt rags. He kicked at them, and was surprised when his foot hit something solid. He realised it must be the Guy which had appeared on top of the fire earlier as it wore a clown mask. Then he noticed the singed blonde hair. Had someone been stupid enough to duck under the safety rope to get a closer look? Something made him bend down to remove the mask and he gasped when he saw a lifeless face staring back at him. Despite her clothes being charred and black, somehow the face had remained untouched by the fire. Joe recognised her at once as his neighbour's daughter, Sally.

Cooke was walking along the Algarve beach he knew so well, looking forward to an ice-cold beer at his favourite bar, and could almost smell the sardines cooking on the barbecue when he was rudely awoken by his mobile. When the phone rang in the early hours it was never good news. He glanced blearily at the clock. Two thirty – the wee small hours, indeed.

"DCI Cooke," he muttered without looking to see who it was, and heard Golding's voice in response.

"Sorry to call you at this hour but we have a nasty one here at the community centre in Frogwell. Young woman, badly burnt and it looks like foul play. I think you ought to come."

"I'll be right there," he replied.

Alice turned over as he climbed out of bed, looked at the clock and then at him.

"Sorry, love, that was Golding, I've got to go out. Try and get back to sleep."

Although they had been married for fifteen years, the night-time calls still distressed her. It always meant that some poor soul had been badly hurt or killed. Sleep wouldn't come easy if at all.

Cooke entered the dark streets of the sleepy village. The community centre was easy to find, being the only building lit up at this hour of the morning. He could see a glow from inside a forensic tent some two hundred yards across the field and made his way towards it. Tom Golding spotted him and came to meet him.

"A local girl, found by the caretaker. Her clothes are badly burnt but remarkably, apart from one small burn on her chin, her face remains virtually untouched. At first it looked like a nasty accident, as though she'd gone under the safety rope for some reason or other and got too near the fire."

"So what makes you think that's not what happened?"

"The fact that she has been identified as Sally Green, who has been missing for three days. Bellingham is looking at the body right now."

"I'll go and have a word."

"The caretaker and a few villagers are in the hall. I was about to go and speak to them."

"I'll be over shortly."

Cooke put on shoe covers and walked towards the tent.

"Any news for me yet?" he called from the doorway.

"Clothes and body are badly burnt so I won't know much until I get her back to the lab but one thing I can tell you, and that is it wasn't the fire that killed her."

CHAPTER 23

Monday 7th November

Having being summoned from his den by a call from the front desk, Cooke found the young lady sitting alone in the small, friendly interview room, nervously twisting her shoulder-length dark hair. A plastic vending cup of hot chocolate was going cold on the table in front of her.

"Hello, Miss Bull, I'm Detective Chief Inspector Cooke," he said in a reassuring tone. "I believe you have some information for us?"

Two heavily made-up eyes looked up at him. Cooke felt it a shame that a pretty girl should feel the need to hide behind such a mask.

"Yes," she said barely above a whisper.

"You were a friend of Sally Green, and I'm told you were with her on the night she disappeared."

"Yes, we were at the village pub quiz. We meet there every Wednesday, Sally, Gina and me."

"So what can you tell me about the evening Sally went missing?"

"She told me she was coming to the police station the next day to tell you who she saw talking to that woman that was murdered."

"Did she tell you who it was?"

"She wouldn't because she didn't want to speak ill of someone in case it wasn't relevant. She did say it was someone we both knew and that he lived in our village."

"Did anyone else hear her tell you this?"

"No. I don't know, maybe. I didn't notice."

"So what happened after the quiz?"

"We all walked as far as the church together like we usually do and said goodbye to Sally there. She only lives a couple of houses down Church Street and Gina and I both live near each other on the Springfield estate."

"Did you hear anything or see anyone after you left her?"

"A few cars passed us but it was foggy. We thought we heard one behind us and moved onto the side of the road because there's no footpath, but when we looked there wasn't anything coming. We didn't think anything of it at the time."

"Thank you for coming to see us, Miss Bull. What you've told us could be very helpful. How can we contact you if we need to speak to you again?"

He wrote down the address and phone number she gave him and saw her out.

Back at his desk he read how PCs Truman and Milner had been on house to house this morning and had spoken to one resident who lived opposite the church and had heard a noise like a car door slamming outside. He'd just watched the news and was getting ready for bed so it was shortly after 10.30. He had looked out of the window and seen the tail lights of a car moving off at speed round the corner into Church Street. He couldn't see the car properly due to the fog but felt that there was something wrong with the rear nearside light as if part of the red lens was missing.

Cooke picked up his phone and dialled Wendy's extension.

"How are you getting on with tracking Valerie's step-brother on the traffic cameras?"

"He came out of the pub and went in the same direction that Valerie went, which was in the opposite direction to his home, but after a few miles he hasn't show up on any cameras in the area."

"Keep on it. He can't have vanished into thin air."

Sharon arrived at Frogwell Community Centre and, after donning the obligatory over-shoe protection, went to see forensics who were still gathering evidence from the site. She was about to duck under the blue tape when she was met by one of the team.

"We've found evidence of a small vehicle entering the field from over there." He pointed to the far end. "There's a gateway which opens out onto a farm track, and we've got some really good tyre prints on the ground there where it was sodden from the recent rain."

"It would explain why nobody saw the vehicle if it didn't enter through the car park as was thought."

"Plenty of footprints by the fire, but none that were of any use as too many people would have been treading there preparing the site in the days preceding the 5th."

"Thanks."

Sharon decided to leave the car and walk to the caretaker's house. After introducing herself she was ushered into the small cottage sitting room which reminded her of her grandmother's house. One wall was occupied by a large dark wood unit where shelves above the cupboards displayed different knick-knacks among framed photos of younger family members. There was a log fire burning in a dark tiled hearth, and a large clock ticked loudly on the mantelpiece next to a brass letter rack stuffed with opened envelopes.

Sharon was waved to the green faux leather sofa as Joe Richards took a mismatched brown velour chair pulled up close to the hearth.

"I'd like to ask you a bit about Bonfire night," Sharon began carefully, aware that the caretaker was exhibiting signs of shock.

"I still can't believe it. That poor young girl," Joe shook his head.

"Were you in charge of setting up the fireworks?"

"No, I only put up the ropes to stop anybody from getting on the grass. Normally they would have been allowed a bit nearer to the fire, but I didn't want loads of feet trampling on the turf and turning it into a mud bath."

"When did you cordon it off?"

"About lunchtime, after the lads had set up the frames for the fireworks."

"Did you notice the guy on top of the bonfire when you were there at lunchtime?"

"Can't say that I did - although it might have been there."

"So who was there setting up the framework?"

"Vic Cash, he's the chairman's brother and he always comes to make any framework necessary for the display. Doesn't charge us either as he can mainly use off cuts from jobs he's done. A couple of the committee were helping him, Gordon Stokes and Chris Atherton."

"On the night, who would have been lighting the fireworks?"

"Gordon and Chris - that's why they were involved with setting it up."

"Where could I find them?"

"They both live on the new estate, but I don't know their addresses. You'd best ask Betty, the secretary; she'll know. She lives at the old forge, on the corner by the village shop."

Sharon thanked him and went back to retrieve her car from the community centre. She drove down to the forge but there was no one home. It was getting dusky and she wanted to discuss her afternoon with Cooke, so decided to head back to base and get uniform to follow up on speaking to the secretary and the two pyrotechnicians.

She arrived back at the station to find Cooke had already left for the day, having been called to collect Alice from the hospital, where it had been necessary to administer drops at her scheduled eye appointment rendering her unable to drive herself home.

CHAPTER 24

Wednesday 9th November

Sharon was updating Cooke on the latest development at Frogwell.

"They've found tyre marks of a small car which has entered through a gate at the far end of the field, and it looks as though it stopped near the back of the bonfire, out of sight of any of the houses near the community centre. Could be how the body was transported to site."

"What other reason would anyone want to use that route?"

"The two men who were lighting fireworks would have come from the village end as they both live there. That gate opens out onto a farm track which ultimately leads to the Wellsend road where the guy who set up the wooden framework is from; and wait for it – he's none other than Mister Victor Cash."

"So he'd be aware of the entrance and would know the site and where he could dispose of the body out of view. I think we need to invite Mr Cash in for another little chat. Ask Greaves to send a couple of his lads to escort him in to help with our enquiries."

"Good morning, Mr Cash. Thank you for agreeing to come in and talk to us."

"I didn't have much choice. I've already told you I didn't know that woman."

"I'd like to ask you about the Bonfire Party at Frogwell on the fifth of November."

"What?" Cash frowned.

"I believe you helped set up the apparatus for the fireworks."

"I always do. My brother's on the committee."

"Did you know Sally Green?"

"No. Why?" The penny dropped. "She wasn't the girl that got burned that night, was she?"

"You can see how it looks. You're seen on more than one occasion in Ashthorp close to where our first victim was staying; then, on the very day you are working on site at the Frogwell community centre, Sally Green ends up on the bonfire."

Cash jumped up shouting, "I have not murdered anyone," banging his fist on the desk with almost every syllable, causing his flabby jowls to wobble.

"Calm down, Mr Cash."

Cash stared at him with a look of pure hatred and for a moment Cooke thought he was going to hit him and was ready to take evasive action, but Cash obviously thought better of it, took a deep breath and sat down.

"I'm telling you I did not know either of the women and had nothing to do with their deaths."

"So you wouldn't mind if we took a look at your car?"

Cash shifted in his chair and didn't answer straight away. "You won't find anything to link me to either woman because I didn't know them."

"So, if you agree, it will help to prove that neither has been in your car."

Cash agreed.

"I'd like you to stay here in case I want to speak to you again."

"Well, well, Mr Cash, it seems that our team have found something really interesting in the boot of your car," Cooke said as he entered the room again a while later.

"You can't have, I didn't know them women and they've never been in my car."

"You're right, nothing was found to suggest that they had."

Cash looked puzzled.

"What we did find is a sapphire and diamond ring identical to one stolen from Councillor Booth's home a couple of weeks ago. Can you explain how it got there?"

"My missus lost her engagement ring a while back."

"Nice try, but the engraving on the inside of the ring matches that on the one which was stolen."

Cash knew that the game was up on his light-fingered escapade and looked down at his hands which were tightly woven together on the desk between them.

Cooke broke the ensuing silence, "I think when I obtain a warrant to search your home, I will find a lot more goods from that list."

Cash was escorted to a cell while Cooke and Sharon returned to their office.

"It could explain why his vehicle was seen on numerous occasions. He's got a quick temper though and I still wouldn't rule him out completely for the recent deaths," Cooke told her.

Sharon agreed. "I've been thinking. If the deaths are linked, which we think they are, and Sally was killed because she was coming to name someone, it's possible she might have discussed it with a work colleague. I'm going over there to see if there was anyone on the staff who she might have confided in."

The dark sky threatened more rain – it was too early for snow, wasn't it? Sharon noticed the clouds of fluttering leaves caught in the strengthening breeze as she drove into town. She parked as near to the store as possible and glanced at its windows, which were already festooned in their Christmas display. At the end of the month the town lights would be turned on and the shoppers would be out in their droves. Sharon loved this time of year and from the moment the clocks went back always looked forward to seeing the brightly lit Christmas trees and other decorations.

The wind was cold, and it was a joy to feel the warmth on her face as she opened the door to the shop. She showed her ID to the lad on the cash desk and asked if she could speak to the manager. Unable to leave his post he called to a colleague, who appeared from the stock room behind him, and asked her to fetch the manager, then smiled at a customer who was ready to pay for a box set of children's books.

Mr Bartlett was soon located and invited her to accompany him to his desk on the mezzanine overlooking the shop floor.

"Is this about Sally?" he asked.

"Partly. I wanted to ask you if she said anything to you about who she had seen Mrs Lawrence speaking to?"

"I'm afraid not, I asked but she told me she didn't want to speak to anyone but the police in case she was wrong and she got someone she knew into trouble."

"You gave her the morning off to come and speak to us but as you know she didn't turn up, and we think it's possible that someone wanted to prevent her telling us what she knew. Is it possible she'd seen her speaking to one of the staff?"

"All the staff are female, except the lad on the cash desk and he's only come back from sick leave this week. Poor lad broke his leg playing football."

"So the only males here would be him and

yourself?"

"Yes, and I can assure you that I have no recollection of talking to the unfortunate woman."

"Is there anyone on the staff that she was particularly friendly with?"

"She often used to go out at lunchtime with Trish, to the shops or somewhere to eat."

"Is Trish in today?"

"She is. Would you like to speak to her?"

"Yes, please."

"Wait here, I'll go and get her."

Sharon looked around the shop floor from her vantage point and saw Bartlett speaking to a woman of about forty who was setting up a display of books near a poster proclaiming that an author would be in store and signing her book the following Wednesday. The woman glanced up at her and started towards the stairs.

"Hello. Mr Bartlett says you'd like to speak to me," Trish said as she walked towards the desk.

"Yes, take a seat."

Once Trish was comfortable, Sharon said, "I believe you were friends with Sally Green?"

"I like to think so. She came here straight from school and I took her under my wing. She was painfully shy and I tried to look out for her. Once she'd emerged from her shell she really blossomed. She was a proper bookworm and this place was a perfect environment for her. She was so good with the customers and had a great sense of humour, as well as a vivid imagination. She often liked to make up stories about customers from the books they bought. I told her more than once she was a natural storyteller."

"Did she tell you that she was coming to speak to us about someone she saw Valerie Lawrence speaking to?"

"No, she didn't say a thing, but looking back she did seem to have had something on her mind last week."

"Do you often have author signings here?" Sharon asked and pointed at the poster.

"Not often. They're a lot of work for everyone. That one's written a romantic novel set in the local area in the 1920s so is more likely to be of interest to our regular client base. We had a chap promoting his first novel last month. I'm so glad I was on holiday that week because apparently he was a friend of Mr Bartlett's and he was fussing more than usual."

"Thank you, Trish. If you think of anything she might have said that could be relevant please give me a call. " Sharon took a card from her bag and gave it her.

They walked to the shop floor together, and while Trish went back to her display, Sharon went to seek out the manager with a view to asking him about last month's author. When she couldn't find him, she went back to the cash desk, where the lad was sitting on a tall breakfast bar-style stool.

"I'm sorry but he's gone to a meeting, and we aren't expecting him back today."

"Can you ask him to ring me please?" Sharon handed him her card.

The drive back to headquarters gave Sharon chance to think, and when she reached base she was keen to speak to Cooke about her theory.

"The book we found among Valerie's things at the Watson house was signed, wasn't it?"

"Yes, by Jason someone-or-other."

"What if it was him who was signing books at Chapter & Verse on the Wednesday and Sally saw Valerie Lawrence speaking to him."

"You have to speak to the author when they are signing their book for you, so what if she did? I expect he spoke to a lot of people that day."

"Her colleague said that the author was a friend of the manager – who's actually the owner of the shop. If it was a local man, Sally might have known him. I couldn't speak to the manager again, but I've asked them to get him to ring me."

CHAPTER 25

Thursday 10th November

A warning light on the dash meant Sharon had to visit Tyre Emporium to check for a possible slow puncture. Fortunately they were quiet and were of the opinion that the sensor was very sensitive and had detected a minimal drop in pressure so she was soon on her way again, albeit rather late. She cursed when her favourite Coldplay song on the radio was replaced by the insistent ringing of her mobile and took the call on hands-free, recognising Bartlett by his rather distinctive squeaky voice.

"Thank you for ringing. Hang on a minute while I pull over."

She drew in alongside the kerb and reached across to her bag for a note pad and pen.

"I needed to ask you the name of the author who was signing books in your shop last month."

"That was Jason Partridge."

"I believe he is a friend of yours?"

"Not actually a friend. I went to school with him. He's had a run of bad luck over the past few years, and when he asked if I'd promote his self-published book I agreed to help him out. He provided the books and came to sign them. It was a lot of work for little return but if it has gone some way to setting him back on track then it was worth it."

"You say he's had a string of bad luck; could you elaborate?"

"Some years ago his wife left him; there were rumours that she'd been seeing someone for some time. His mother came to live with him and his kiddie, who must have been about eleven at the time. He'd always liked a bet on the horses but it sounds like he became addicted and got himself into serious debt through his gambling. Everyone knows that's a mug's game and the only winner is the bookie. His mother died, leaving him and the boy to cope. Fortunately for him he inherited her house which she had been renting out, intending to move back once the lad left school and she was no longer needed. He was able to pay off his debts and help put his lad through university. When he was made redundant earlier in the year, he decided to finish a book he started years ago and self-publish it, which is when he asked me about arranging the signing."

"What sort of book was it?"

"A modern romance was how he described it. Quite a popular genre with the ladies."

"I think that's all. Thank you for your help."

Sharon found Cooke reading the full report of

goods found in Cash's garage.

"Cash has admitted to the burglaries and had now signed a statement to that effect but is still adamant that he had nothing to do with the deaths, and with only circumstantial
evidence against him I've had to let him go."

"The bookstore owner phoned me on my way in and told me his friend Jason Partridge was the author. He had run up quite a gambling debt a few years back, but a legacy paid that off and he seems to have turned his life around."

"Cash is looking less likely but we still have the brother and husband in the picture. Neither has an alibi that can be checked out."

"But why would either of them want to kill Sally Green?"

"Perhaps her death has nothing to do with the first case."

Wendy popped her head round the door.

"I've got that full list of red Corsas in the area you asked for." She came in and handed a printout to Cooke.

"Thanks, Wendy." Cooke was surprised there were so many. He quickly scanned down the list and tapped it with his forefinger. "I know that name. Where have I heard it before?"

Cooke handed the list back to Wendy.

"Punch these names into the computer, see what you can find out about each owner, try and narrow down the search."

Certain he'd heard that name recently, Cooke

reached over and picked up the case file and started to flick through the reports.

"Here it is! Fred Hammond was one of the golfer lads, but not the one who actually found the body in the bunker. He gave an address in Frogwell, which could also link him to the second death. I think we need to have a chat with him pronto."

"No point in going until this evening, he's bound to be at work," Sharon replied.

"You're probably right."

Cooke parked behind a relatively new red Corsa almost outside the terraced house on a small estate, built in the Sixties with street names taken from local historical icons. Flanked by homes with well-kept gardens, this house was decidedly neglected. They walked through the open gate and Sharon took in the overgrown lawn and weed-covered beds where a couple of late roses struggled to brighten things up. They approached the wooden door, where dark green paint flaked around a dirty pane of glass.

She stood back as Cooke hammered on the tarnished brass knocker which summoned someone who could be heard bounding down the stairs. The door opened and they were confronted by a young man who she put in his early twenties.

"Mr Hammond, we are DCI Cooke and DI Whitaker of Riversmeet Police," They both showed their ID. "We've met before, I believe, at Wellsend golf course."

"That's right, I recognise you now," Hammond replied.

"We'd like a word with you. Could we come in?"

"Yes, but I told your officers everything I could on the day."

He showed them through to a nicely furnished, if rather untidy, living room. Cooke noticed a pile of papers next to the hearth, where an electric fire stood, and judging from the amount of dust on it he assumed it was only there for decoration.

"Do you live here alone?" Cooke asked.

"No, with my dad."

Once they were seated it didn't take long to realise there was no heating on in the house as it seemed even colder than it was outside. Cooke could see his breath and rubbed his hands together and wished he'd been wearing his overcoat. He'd teased Sharon, all togged up complete with scarf and gloves when they left the office.

"I believe you are the owner of the Red Vauxhall outside?"

"The Corsa, yes, at least it will be mine once I've finished paying it off. I sometimes have to work at other depots and needed something reliable."

"Where do you work?"

"At the Vauxhall dealership in Riversmeet."

"Can you tell me if you knew the woman that you and your mates found on the golf course that day?"

"Never seen her before."

"You're sure of that?"

"Positive."

"Where were you on the night of Friday, the seventh of October?"

"Friday night is boys' night so I'd have been at the pub – the Cat and Fiddle in the high street. Why?"

"So there would be people there who would verify this?"

"Yes. I'm always there on a Friday night – ask anyone."

"Where were you on the evening of Wednesday, the second of November?"

"Wednesday night is quiz night at the same pub so I would have been there."

"You know Sally Green?"

"Pretty girl. I can't believe I'll never see her again."

"Did you see her that night?"

"Yes, her team beat us by one point."

"Did you see her after the quiz?"

"She and her mates stayed for a while but left before us."

Hammond paled as he realised he was being asked about two different women who had both been killed.

"I don't like this. First you ask me about a stranger who turns up dead on the golf course, and now you're asking me about Sally. Surely you can't think I know anything about what happened to them."

"If you've done nothing wrong you have

nothing to worry about."

CHAPTER 26
Friday 11th November

"We've got lots of reasons to suspect Fred Hammond, but it's all circumstantial. He was at the golf club when Valerie Lawrence's body was found but denies knowing her. He knew Sally Green, but we've said before that her death might have nothing to do with the first. He has a red Corsa but so have Cash and the barman at the golf course, who Wendy was going to see this morning."

"It'll be interesting to hear what Golding has uncovered too," Sharon replied as they entered the main office for the late morning meeting.

The general hubbub died down as Cooke took up position by the far wall.

"Wendy, what info do you have for us on the golf club barman?"

"He wasn't on the rota to work on the Friday night and says he was at his in-laws' twenty-fifth wedding anniversary party in Leeds. He showed me photos of the event on his phone. I've spoken to his wife who has verified this, and I'll check with her parents on Monday when they come back from their celebratory cruise."

"Tom, any more luck with yours?"

"One tells me he was in hospital for an operation at the time of the first murder – I still have to check that out; the other had an early night after helping at his daughter's tenth birthday party."

Jimmy raised his hand.

"Yes, Jimmy?"

"The list from her telephone provider came through just now. I haven't had chance to study it yet."

"Excellent! Get onto that straight after this meeting."

Cooke wrote a new name on the board then turned to address the others.

"Fred Hammond who Sharon and I spoke to yesterday; he was one of the lads who found the body on the golf course and coincidently drives a red Corsa. Add that to the fact that he lives in the same village as Sally Green, and he becomes a person of interest. As yet we have nothing else to connect him with Valerie Lawrence, who he insists he did not know."

"And no obvious motive." Golding remarked.

"Money may be a problem. He lives with his father and there was no heating on in the house when we visited him early evening which may indicate they are struggling, and although I can't see that as a motive, it wouldn't hurt to have a look at his finances, Wendy."

"Will do."

"He works at the Vauxhall dealership in town. Tom, have a word with his boss; see what you can find out about him."

"Sharon, go and have a chat with Sally Green's parents. If her death has nothing to do with the first we need to look into any old boyfriends or anyone she may have fallen out with."

"We'll compare notes later – say three thirty." Cooke took his car keys from his pocket and Sharon gave him questioning look.

"Alice has got the day off, so I think I'll take her to the Cat and Fiddle and see what they have to offer for lunch."

As it happened Alice had already made other arrangements when he phoned her from the car park, so he went alone and thus arrived a little earlier than planned. The door was unlocked so he walked into the bar, which seemed to be deserted, and called out. The round face of a man with a mess of curly hair appeared above the bar.

"We're not open until twelve."

Cooke showed his warrant and introduced himself. "Are you the landlord?"

"Bob Wright, yes, it's my name above the door."

"I'd like to have a little chat about one of your regulars."

"Take a seat over by the fire. I just need to finish putting on the new barrel of bitter so I can get the trap door closed before the staff start arriving. Don't want anyone falling down into the cellar by accident." With that he vanished again from sight.

Cooke noticed that the only offerings for lunch were meat pies or one of the sad looking ready-made sandwiches languishing in a glass display unit on the bar and was glad he hadn't brought Alice here. He decided that fish and chips from Fryer Tuck would be favourite. He was grateful that the fire was lit and warmed his hands before sitting in the little nook nearby to take in the rest of the traditional old bar. There was a bar billiards table at the far end of the room. He hadn't seen one for years and remembered hours playing the game in his youth. He noticed one windowsill was stacked with dominoes, packs of cards and cribbage boards and an alcove on the other side of the huge stone hearth housed a darts board. There was an oil painting of the pub above the fire, which must have been there for some years as it still bore the yellow filter of nicotine from the days before smoking was banned.

"Can I get you a drink?" a voice boomed from the bar area.

"No, thanks."

The landlord strode over. "This is no doubt to do with poor Sally Green. I've already told your lads everything I could remember about the quiz night."

"It's not about the quiz night. It's a Friday night I'm more interested in. Friday 7th October."

"Games night, or as the locals call it, boys' night. It's become quite a tradition over the years. The wives go to bingo at the community centre on a Thursday night and the chaps stay in to look after the kids and earn their free pass for a Friday night. The younger lads come too and if they have a girlfriend they join them later."

"Fred Hammond tells me he's a regular here of a Friday night."

"Fred? Since he came back from university he's never missed a Friday night."

"So he would have been here on Friday 7th October?"

"Definitely."

"Does he have a girlfriend?"

"I don't think so. He did bring a new lady in about a month ago, but I haven't seen her since."

"What was she like?"

"She was blonde, but to be honest I didn't get a very good look at her, I didn't serve them and they went to sit out in the garden."

The door opened and an elderly man walked in and looked around the bar before seeing the landlord sitting with Cooke, and nodded at them by way of acknowledgement.

"Morning, Walt," the landlord said to the newcomer, then told Cooke, "This is Walt, my oldest regular, and I'm sitting on his chair, so I'd better go and get him his stout."

The old boy sat in the recently vacated chair and scowled at Cooke before stating, "You're not a local."

Bob interrupted, "This here's a detective. He's asking about a Friday night last month."

Cooke looked towards the speaker and saw chalked on the big blackboard beside the bar that it was cribbage night tonight, and asked the old man if there was a game every Friday.

"No, just once a month. Last one was a month ago against the Dog & Bone."

"Would that have been on the fourteenth?"

"Sounds about right if it was the second Friday. First Friday is darts, second crib, third whist and fourth dominoes," the old boy counted then off on his fingers.

"Would Fred Hammond have played in any of these?"

"Aye, plays every week. He's a good all-rounder, but really good with the arrows. Always picked to play in the team."

"So he would have been playing last month?"

"Never missed a game."

"And if darts is the first Friday in the month that would have been the seventh, right?"

"Aye, sounds right."

The landlord who had been listening to the conversation as he poured the bottled beer carefully into a glass added, "Last month he left straight after his game and didn't even accept a winner's pint from old Harry Simms."

"Aye, you're right, Bob. Said he didn't feel well."

"What time would that have been?" Cooke

addressed this to the landlord.

"He always played second on the oche so it would have been quite early in the evening."

Cooke got up to leave.

"Well, it's been nice speaking to you, gentlemen. Must get on."

One large haddock and chips later and suitably sated, Cooke went to find out what the others had discovered.

Golding kicked off. "Fred Hammond is a well-respected member of staff. A university graduate, he had actually wanted to work in a sports environment but came back home to live with his father – they think to keep a roof over the old man's head. He is a good salesman and earns commission on top of his monthly salary."

"So his finances are good, Wendy?"

"He manages to stay out of the red and does most of his spending by card. There is a regular amount going out to a finance company for the car, direct debit for electricity and a small cash withdrawal every week."

"I've been to his local to check out his alibi and he was there on the Friday night but left early, so may still have had time to pick up Valerie at the station. He also visited the pub with a blonde about a month ago."

"Sharon, what have you got on Sally Green?"

"Her mum says she has had a couple of boyfriends but nothing serious. One had moved away and the other has now set up home with someone else. I mentioned Fred Hammond and she would have known him, but they really would have had nothing in common. Sally was a shy girl who was happiest with her nose in a book."

"Do we have enough to get Hammond in for questioning?" asked Golding.

"We have no evidence that he knew Valerie Lawrence and no obvious motive, so I don't think we have."

CHAPTER 27
Saturday 12th November

Saturday morning dawned, but with his superiors breathing down Cooke's neck and still no real breakthrough there could be no let up in searching for the vital clue. His team were tired and he'd allowed them a lie-in, so they were making a later start today. He decided to call in at his favourite patisserie on the way into work this morning and put in an order to be delivered in time for the 11am meeting.

Sharon arrived soon after him and they were discussing the main suspects again when a knock preceded Wendy's entrance. "Excuse me, sir, but Janice from human resources just popped in to see me and brought this." She held up a hard-back book. "She'd been looking for something to read on holiday so I told her about a crime series I'd started to read and offered to lend her the first book. I told her I'd leave it on my desk and I have to say I was a bit annoyed when she never came to pick it up before she went away. However, it seems she took this one by mistake. I'd been flicking through it before packing it up with Valerie Lawrence's belongings and must have forgotten to put it with the rest. Do you think I need to send it? It looks like a chick lit and I can't imagine Mr Lawrence wanting to read it."

"Can I look at it?" Sharon held out her hand. "Jason Partridge, yes – that's the author who was doing the book signing at Chapter& Verse."

She turned the book over to read the summary of the story and gasped as she saw the author's photo on the back.

"That's Giles Hammond. I thought I'd seen him somewhere before. Jason Partridge must be his pen name. Giles Hammond and Valerie Lawrence were on the same holiday together in Italy earlier this year."

"Hot Nights in Tuscany," Wendy added. " Janice said it was rather raunchy."

Sharon looked inside the book at the page where the author had signed and read, *To Val with lots of love G* followed by the author's official signature.

Sharon showed Cooke. "I'm more convinced than ever that there was more between them on that holiday than he led me to believe."

"Hammond?" Cooke looked at Sharon. "Are you thinking what I'm thinking?"

"Yes."

"Do you have Giles Hammond's address?"

"No - I only had a list of phone numbers from the tour company."

Sharon went to her desk drawer and took out the printout from Tour2Explore Holidays and began to dial their number. After a brief chat with the manager, she looked at Cooke.

"Same address – he must be Fred's father!"

"We have a link now between Fred and Giles Hammond and my guess is that Fred did know Valerie Lawrence and that it was him that was seen talking to her at the station."

"Is everyone in, Wendy?"

"Yes."

"Come on then, it's almost eleven. Let's go and speak to the others."

Cooke went via the front desk to collect his order and carried the sumptuous selection through to the main office where he placed it on an empty desk in the corner.

"Get yourselves a drink and help yourselves to a pastry," he told the team, and walked over to the white board to wait for them to return to their seats.

Sharon fastened a photocopy she'd made of the image from the back of the book to the board and Cooke began to speak.

"I think we've had a bit of a breakthrough. This is Giles Hammond, aka Jason Partridge, author. He knew Valerie Lawrence and despite his denial, we think there was something going on between them. His book, which Sharon is holding, was among her possessions and has only just come to light. It's dedicated to her, with love. We know that he ran up a large gambling debt some time ago but paid it off with a legacy, and according to his old school friend at the book shop, he'd seen the error of his ways and had given up betting. He's out of work and the son is doing his best to keep them afloat with his wages from a car dealership. We now know that Fred Hammond, who drives a red Corsa, is his son so we have a link between the lad and Valerie. He had time to get from the darts game to the station and could very well be the person she was seen talking to."

"Maybe he knew about the affair and was trying to blackmail her," Wendy suggested.

"Possibly. I think we need to look at Hammond senior too. Jimmy, we have a mobile number for him but Sharon couldn't get an answer on it. Can you find out if there is a new number allocated to him?

"Wendy, have a look at the father's finances.

"Tom, I think he could be back on the slippery gambling slope, so see what you can find out from the local bookies."

"He might be doing it online," Tom pointed out.

"True, but he hasn't got a job. When I was speaking to the son the other day I noticed a pile of Racing Posts, and that isn't a cheap paper; why spend out on it if he could get all the necessary information online? No, I think he's more likely to spend his afternoon watching the horses in the warmth of the bookies than at home because the house is like a freezer. Any questions?"

No one replied.

"All back here at two thirty."

"Jimmy, any news on another mobile?" Cooke asked.

"There is a pay as you go sim registered to him which he seems to have used intermittently, and his number matches some of the recent calls uncovered on Valerie's other phone."

"So he'd definitely been in touch with her while she was here. Wendy, what about Hammond senior's financial situation?"

"Giles Hammond has a regular income from his Job Seekers allowance but his account has been getting further and further into the red with outgoings and regular trips to the ATM, meaning he's topped out on his agreed overdraft. It seems the son is bearing the brunt of the household expenses as there are no direct debits on the account for any household services."

"How did you get on with the gambling angle, Tom?"

"He spends every afternoon in a privately owned betting shop in Stonewell. The owner, one 'Lucky' Jim Young tells me he doesn't bet high stakes but must spend in the region of fifty quid a week."

"So he's in financial trouble again. His mother's unfortunate death pulled him out of the mire last time. Looks like he's spent his inheritance and is now back to square one making money the most likely motive."

"But Valerie's will leaves everything to her husband. He couldn't gain by killing her," Golding pointed out.

"Perhaps she had something on him and threatened to disclose it. Maybe his mother's death wasn't an accident," Wendy added.

"It's possible. Look into it; see if there was any doubt about her death at the time."

"Boss!" Jimmy shouted.

All eyes turned to him.

"I sent the railway station footage to a mate of mine who has got some really sophisticated tech and he's sent me this photo. You can just about make out the licence plate of the Corsa."

A check against the list confirmed that it belonged to Fred Hammond.

"The father and son may be in this together?" Golding asked.

"I think we need to bring them both in. Fred should be at work. Sharon and I will go and collect him first. Tom, once we've got him safely in an interview room, I want you and Jimmy to go and winkle Hammond senior out of the bookies. I want to make sure we keep them apart, not give them any chance to compare notes. Wendy, apply for warrants to search the lad's Vauxhall and his father's car too. "

CHAPTER 28

Saturday 12th November

The aroma of beef casserole filled the house when Cooke popped home en route to the car franchise and found Alice enjoying her afternoon cuppa.

"That smells good," Cooke said, "but I have a feeling I will be very late home tonight."

"Okay, if you are I can have a pizza and we can have the casserole warmed up another day. It often tastes even better when it's had time to rest."

Cooke kissed her on the cheek and left again.

When they arrived at the car showroom Cooke and Sharon were greeted by a middle-aged, suited man eager to help them. The shark's smile vanished when they showed their IDs.

"We'd like to speak to Fred Hammond."

"He's with a customer at the moment finalising some paperwork. There's nobody in the waiting room so you can go in there and I'll send him in as soon as he's done. There's a free drinks machine – help yourselves to whatever you fancy."

At least it was warm in the waiting room and both, ignoring the vending machine, took seats next to a coffee table strewn with magazines and car brochures. There was a television playing with the sound down and Cooke found himself watching rugby while Sharon picked up a brochure and flicked idly through it.

Fred Hammond wore a worried face as he walked through the door.

"You want to speak to me?"

"Yes, due to receiving more information, we'd like you to come to the police station with us to answer some further questions."

"Am I under arrest?"

"We'd just like you to help with our enquiries. The interview will be recorded so you may like to have a solicitor with you."

"I don't have a solicitor, and I've done nothing wrong, so I won't need one."

Sharon turned on the tape and named those present. Cooke took the lead.

"You have previously told us that you did not know Valerie Lawrence. We have reason to believe that you did."

"I didn't know her and that's the honest truth."

"You have told us that you were at the pub on Friday 7th October."

"As I said, I always go to boys' night on a Friday."

"I am told you left early that night."

Fred thought for a minute and replied, "Yes, I did. I wasn't feeling very well – thought it was the chicken 'cause it had been in the fridge for a while.

Thankfully after a good night's sleep I felt better in the morning."

"What time did you leave the pub?"

"I was on second and left straight after my game so about quarter to eight I guess."

"Did you drive to the pub?"

"No, I walked as I always have a few pints on a Friday night."

"Where did you go?"

"I went home to bed."

"So your car would have been outside your home all evening?"

"It should have been, but I found a note when I got home. Dad had borrowed it and I was furious because he wasn't back the next morning, and I ended up having to drive his old banger to meet up with my mates – so embarrassing."

"Does he often borrow your car?"

"Once before when he wanted to make a good impression. He had it for a couple of days, and promised it would be the only time, as he'd soon be able to pay his way. At least he had the decency to ask that time."

"Did he tell you where he'd been this time?"

"I didn't ask. It was the last straw and the reason why I've washed my hands of him. He doesn't deserve my help. The man's a loser, wasted a good part of his redundancy on a bloody holiday and the rest on the nags. The business at the golf course really upset me and when I came home to a cold empty house I saw red. I packed a bag and drove round to my mate's flat and I've been sleeping on his sofa ever since. You were lucky to catch me at the house the other day. I went round to collect some more of my stuff when I knew the old man would be out."

"Did you drive to work this morning?"

"Yes."

"Could I have your keys please? I've applied for a warrant to search the vehicle."

"I don't understand. You can't possibly think– "

"You may not have known Valerie Lawrence, but your father certainly did."

Fred handed over his keys.

"Just one last question. You went to the Cat and Fiddle about a month ago with a blonde lady, can you tell me who it was?"

"Not that it's anyone's business, but it was Emilia Nelson, a friend of mine from university."

"And she would verify this?"

"Yes. Ring her if you have to."

Cooke took down her phone number.

"Someone will be in to take your fingerprints for elimination purposes."

Cooke motioned Sharon to turn off the tape and went out to phone Alan Williams to check on what car his mate had arrived in for the golf match. Next he rang the student who confirmed that she had been visiting the area and had caught up with Fred over a drink. Finally he contacted Golding. "I think we can eliminate Fred Hammond now. Arrest Hammond senior for the murder of Valerie Lawrence."

As expected, Giles Hammond's car was parked up near the bookies. Golding and Jimmy found him cheering on Bonttay, in the 16.05 at Cheltenham, which, unfortunately for Mr Hammond, was beaten easily in the final furlong by Queens Gamble. To compound his woes he looked up and saw he had company.

"Giles Hammond, you are under arrest for the murder of Valerie Lawrence. You do not have to say anything but it may harm your defence if you do not mention when questioned something which you later rely on in court. Anything you do say may be given in evidence."

Hammond looked pleadingly at the bookie then at Golding.

"Just because I knew her doesn't mean I killed her. You can't prove that I did. Tell them, Jim, I wouldn't hurt a fly."

Jim, not wanting to get involved, studiously ignored him as he took another punter's winning slip and Jimmy escorted him to their car.

Back at the station Giles Hammond was taken to the least comfortable interview room where he was left awaiting his chosen brief with Smiler, a constable whose stern looks had quickly earned him his nickname.

Sharon nipped out to get some decent coffee and Cooke made his way to the main office where

Wendy was eager to tell him of her findings.

"Mrs Hammond senior had injuries consistent with having fallen down a flight of stairs, a broken leg and arm. A blow on the head had been determined as cause of death which was thought could have been caused by hitting the newel post at the bottom of the stairs and forensics did find blood on it. Although it seemed the most likely scenario there was one member of the forensics team who thought the shape of the wound wasn't quite right."

"So it is possible that it was something else that caused the fatal blow?"

"Yes, but as nothing else was ever found, and there was no reason to think that the death was suspicious, it was recorded as accidental."

"Interesting – good work. Have we got the warrants for searching the cars?"

"Yes."

"Get forensics onto that. Fred Hammond's car is at his place of work and Giles' is outside the bookies in Stonewell."

Cooke left word at the front desk to be informed when Giles Hammond's legal representative arrived and made his way upstairs to find Sharon had already returned and was typing out a statement for the younger Mr Hammond to sign. He told her what Wendy had found out and together they discussed their plan of action for the father.

"If he did help his mother on her way to get

his hands on her money, who knows what he is capable of. I was never happy with Fred being guilty as it would have been a really stupid place to leave the body, knowing he was going to be there the next day," Cooke said.

"I have to say that he really did seem to be telling the truth."

"If he's happy to sign that statement, then I think we should let him go."

With Giles Hammond's lawyer, Nick Peters, now present, Sharon turned on the tape and detailed all present in the interview.

Cooke began. "Mr Hammond, we know that you were on the Tour2Explore Holidays tour of Italy in May of this year and when you spoke to DI Whitaker on –" Cooke looked at the piece of paper in his hand "– October 17th, you said that you had not spoken to any of your holiday companions since that date. We have a copy of your book which you signed for Valerie Lawrence at a promotion held in the book shop, Chapter & Verse, on Wednesday 5th October. "

"I signed quite a few books. I didn't recognise her."

"I think you did have an affair with her on that holiday and that the book may have been inspired by it."

"Rubbish. I started writing it ages ago. There was nothing between us."

"Perhaps Valerie Lawrence confronted you after realising that the story was about your illicit affair. Maybe she threatened to sue you," Cooke said.

"There was no affair," Hammond snapped.

"Mr Hammond has already told you that there was no affair, illicit or other, between him and Mrs Lawrence," Peters calmly pointed out.

Sharon took a piece of paper from the file in front of her and placed it in front of Hammond.

"Do you recognise this telephone number?"

"No."

"It was allocated to you on a pay as you go phone you purchased in August 2011."

"If you say so. I don't remember phone numbers."

Sharon took out another sheet of paper with a list of phone calls made to and from the mobile during the past month.

"On this list the highlighted items are of phone calls between that mobile and the one belonging to Valerie Lawrence during the time between the fifth and seventh of October. What do you have to say about that?"

Hammond stared at the desk as if the answer were there to be found, then looking at Sharon said, "She was pestering me. She saw me in the shop and must have thought it would be fun to be seen with an up-and-coming author. Get her fifteen minutes of fame by proxy."

"Mr Hammond, you have continually lied to

us," Cooke boomed. "First you say you haven't spoken to her, then you tell us you didn't recognise her, and now, even though apart from one call on the Friday evening, there are no others registered from her phone to yours, you are trying to tell us that she was throwing herself at a two-bit unknown author. Give us some credit."

"So why lie to us?" Sharon added.

"Isn't it obvious? She's dead, presumably murdered. I didn't want to be mixed up with it."

"But when I spoke to you on the seventeenth and you told the first lie, you didn't know that."

"Yes, I did – you're just saying that to make me look bad. I've done nothing wrong and you can't prove that I have." With a look of defiance Hammond folded his arms and stared at the wall behind them.

"What were you doing on Friday 7th October?" Cooke resumed the questioning.

"At home watching TV until the news, then I would have gone to bed."

"Whose bed, Mr Hammond? Your son has told us that you were out all night."

"I should be so lucky. He must have got the date wrong"

"He seemed pretty certain as he needed his car the next day and was forced to travel to Wellsend, to play golf with his mates, in your car."

"That was over a month ago. How can I be expected to remember?"

"We'll give you some time to refresh your memory. Interview suspended at twenty thirty-five. Someone will be in to take your fingerprints and you will be taken to your accommodation for the night."

Sharon turned off the tape while Cooke gathered his paperwork and they left their suspect to stew while they awaited news from the search of the son's car.

CHAPTER 29

Sunday 13th November

It had been a long night of fitful sleep and it was still dark when Cooke peered through the living room curtains to see rain hitting the window pane. Six am and awake again, he left Alice snuggled up in a nice cosy bed. The heating hadn't kicked in yet and the house was the damp sort of cold which slowly seeps into your bones. A hot drink and a bowl of porridge was called for.

Despite the fact that it was Sunday and he had to go into work, Cooke was feeling optimistic. Until yesterday the enquiry had been stagnant, but now he was counting on getting the right evidence to prove that Giles Hammond was their man.

Restless, he decided he might as well go into work, get some paperwork done, do something constructive.

The rain had eased off to a fine drizzle as Cooke started the engine and pushed a compilation CD into the player ready to sing along loudly to some rock classics.

Still humming the last song he'd heard as he

opened the door to the station, he was enveloped in the warmth of the central heating. The civilian manning the desk this morning told him it had been a quiet night with only one extra inhabitant in the cells - a man who'd had one too many and taken a swipe at a young lad he'd thought was eyeing up his girlfriend.

As Cooke climbed the stairs he wished he'd picked up a coffee on the way in. He couldn't face going back out so, with a sigh, sat down to make a start.

Good news was preceded by the ringing of his phone. Forensics were on the ball and fingerprints found on the passenger door handle inside the Corsa had been a match to those of Valerie Lawrence proving that she had been inside the vehicle. A lipstick of a similar shade to hers was found under the passenger seat. Fabric fibres and hairs from both cars were still being examined.

Cooke gave Sharon the news when she arrived. Hammond's brief was due back at nine o'clock, and when the desk rang through to say that they were both ready and waiting in the interview room they gathered their paperwork and went to join them.

With the preliminaries attended to, Cooke made a start.

"How's your memory this morning, Mr Hammond?"

"There's nothing wrong with my memory."

"We have a signed statement from your son to say that you borrowed his car the night of 7th

October and that you did not get back by 8am the next morning when he needed it."

"I told you he must have got the date wrong."

"No, he hadn't. We have checked that he did arrive at his destination in a car which fits the description of one Fiesta registered to you."

"But that doesn't prove I had his car the night before. I didn't. I was at home in bed."

"When did you last see Valerie Lawrence?"

"At the book signing."

"And that's the only time you saw her?"

"Yes."

"So can you explain why her fingerprints were found on the door handle inside your son's car, which we know you borrowed on the night she died?"

"Perhaps he gave her a lift or something."

"Is he in the habit of giving strange women a lift?"

"I don't know."

There was a knock at the door and Cooke looked up to see a uniformed officer. "There's a phone call for you, guv."

Cooke left to take the call and resumed the conversation on his return.

"A lipstick found underneath the passenger seat matches the colour of the one Valerie Lawrence was wearing when she was found, where you left her, on the golf course at Wellsend."

"I didn't! Why don't you listen?"

"We also have evidence that Sally Green was

transported in the boot of your car. So stop lying to us and tell the truth. Was Valerie an accident, and you knew Sally had seen you talking to her?"

Hammond didn't answer straight away but looked down at his hands and muttered something to himself.

"Speak up!"

Hammond looked up and growled, "I said they're all liars."

"Who are?"

"Women!"

"So tell us what happened."

"I loved her."

Cooke waited silently for him to resume.

"It was a whirlwind romance, but we never told anyone else on that holiday. She was a widow, I'd lost my wife, we were both free agents and weren't doing anything wrong, but somehow the cloak and dagger aspect made every moment together more special. We were engaged – well, unofficially. I bought her a ring and we planned to meet up the week following the holiday."

"Did you meet up?"

"I couldn't contact her. I only had her mobile number, which she gave me on the last night, but she must have written it down wrong. I knew that she lived in Cheltenham so I travelled down there, and wandered the streets hoping to catch a glimpse of her. I put an ad in the local newspaper asking her to get in touch."

He looked crestfallen as he remembered.

"So did she get in touch?" Cooke prompted.

"No. But she walked back into my life at the book signing. She was amused to be the subject of my novel and I signed a copy for her and gave it to her. I wanted to meet her once the shop closed but she said she was busy and asked me for my number saying she'd ring me when she was free. I was so pleased when she rang on Friday and asked me if I could pick her up from the station. She was wearing the ring I'd bought her, and I was so happy to have her by my side once more. I drove out of town; I'd booked a table at The Greedy Hen, but she said she needed to speak to me first so we stopped at a well-known local viewpoint. It was picture perfect and so romantic with the stars above and the lights of the town below. I leant over to kiss her and she dropped the bombshell. Told me she was married and for her it had only been a holiday fling. She'd told us she was a widow, who had been left comfortably off by her late husband, but it was all lies. I told her I loved her."

Hammond stared into space and seemed in a world of his own.

"So what happened next?" Cooke prompted.

"She laughed. I completely lost it. I wasn't thinking. I grabbed her and shook her. I realised what I'd done and let her go, still hoping this was all a game, but she ran off. I chased her, I still thought I could change her mind. She was fit and was getting away, but she fell and hit her head on a large stone. When I got to her I realised she was unconscious. I picked her up and she wasn't breathing. I panicked and dropped her and she rolled into the bunker."

"So you didn't check if she had a pulse?"

"She wasn't breathing."

"I'm guessing that Sally Green had to be killed before she could tell us."

"Sally knew me and I know she heard me talking to Valerie because she made a comment afterwards. Then as I was going into the pub that night for a swift half, I heard her telling her friend that she was coming to tell the police about what she'd seen and heard. I parked in the pull-in by the church and waited in the churchyard. I didn't intend to harm her, I just wanted to speak to her once she was on her own, tell her she'd got it all wrong, but she wouldn't listen. Women – they never bloody well listen."

CHAPTER 30

Sunday 13th November

Cooke poured two glasses of Merlot and handed one to Alice before settling next to her on the sofa.

"That casserole was delicious," he told her. "Well worth the wait."

"Good to be able to enjoy it together in the knowledge that you have closed that case." Alice raised her glass.

"It was a difficult one. What makes someone tell so many lies?"

"Sometimes it's to hide something. Some people make things up because they don't feel their life is exciting enough, but these things have a way of catching up with them in the end."

"True." Cooke, deep in thought, watched the flames lap around a log in the wood burner for a while before speaking again.

"She was a different person to everyone who knew her, and I don't think we ever found out who the real Valerie was behind the various masks she wore. Maybe it was more about image and what people thought of her."

"Like trying to be the person she thought they would like better?"

"Yes, although ultimately it led to her death."

"What's he being charged with?"

"Her death was a tragic accident. Whether she would have lived if he had helped her or called for help is immaterial. Trying to cover his tracks, he murdered an innocent girl and that is what he'll do time for."

"Would you like a nightcap – a hot chocolate with a dash of brandy?"

"That sounds good."

Alice went to the kitchen to prepare their drinks, and on her return found her husband fast asleep.

THANK YOU

I would like to say a big thank you to the following:

Lorraine Swoboda for your wonderful job of editing this book, your kind suggestions and your impeccable attention to detail
Dawn Johnson for my book cover design and for your eagle-eyed proof reading
My family for your continued support and belief in my writing journey
My chatter chums for listening to my ramblings and for your encouragement
My readers who make it all worthwhile

BOOKS BY THIS AUTHOR

Sweet Smell Of Revenge

Today is all about revenge.
Gloucestershire lorry driver Tony Hedges sets off on the road north, his mind on an unresolved argument with his wife. Within hours all contact with him is lost.
Two days later a boy taking an early morning run on the Derbyshire moors falls across something macabre in a disused quarry. DCI Ben Cooke and his team must identify the human remains found there, and establish whether a crime has been committed.
Is Tony a victim or a suspect? As events unfold, and the past is uncovered, seemingly unconnected lives will be changed forever.

Trick Of The Eye

Love comes in many guises.
Chloe's life is just as she wants it. She has her own

cosy flat, a job she enjoys, and a man who loves her as much as she loves him.

When small incidents happen, she thinks nothing of them. Then her boyfriend is the victim of a hit and run near his home, and she begins to wonder whether something more sinister lies behind the anonymous gifts and messages, the petty vandalism, and the loss of personal items from her home.

What starts as a harmless infatuation turns into a more determined pursuit. Someone wants her for their own, and they aren't going to let anything – or anyone – get in their way.